STURGEON
POINT

EDWARD WEIL

PAGE PUBLISHING, INC.
New York, NY

First originally published by Page Publishing, Inc. 2016

ISBN 978-1-68289-284-8 (pbk)
ISBN 978-1-68289-285-5 (digital)

Printed in the United States of America

It was the first day after the last day of school and that first day of summer break found them. The three high school friends, the same way every Saturday in their recent past had found them, hung over, dry-mouthed, and eyes shot with blood. The clock radio sounded out loud like it did every morning before school. That morning's random radio song, "Stroke Me" by Billy Squier brought them out of their alcohol, marijuana-induced state of coma, making them ask, Why in the world did we set the alarm on a Saturday the first day of summer break?

Cliff pushed several beer cans out of the way, kicked a few more, and spilled the bong on his way to turn off that screaming Billy Squier before his head split in two.

"Get up, you lightweights," yelled Cliff as he turned off the song and searched the fridge for any leftover beers from last night's free-for-all.

Cliff tossed two full beers into the darkness while simultaneously saying, "Think fast, fags. Wake up and drink up! Today is going to be a big day for us!"

Nowhere, not even in his wildest dreams could he have ever imagined that he had just made the biggest understatement of the wildest ride of their lives. If they could have seen into the future, they may have just gone back to sleeping off that hangover, they knew and had grown to expect on Saturday mornings. At the very least, they would have cinched their safety belts, tied down the loose furniture, and let out the cat. For their lives would soon be doing a million miles per hour down a winding gravel country road, holding onto their stomachs, and looking to get off at the very next stop.

Out of the dark room came two yells. Lee yelled, "Ouch! Hey, motherfucker! You just hit me in the face with the beer! What the fuck! Couldn't you wait till I was lookin' or at least completely awake? Shit!"

The second yell was from Freddie. "Jesus H Christ! Cliff, that's my mother fucking head!"

Cliff laughed. "They're cold. Hold them against your face and head and get yourselves up and moving. You're burning daylight, not to mention crying like little girls!" he said as he threw open the front room curtains to let the morning sun in.

"What the fuck. Cliff!" cried Lee. Almost word for word and together, both Lee and Freddie in pissed-off voices said, "It's still fucking dark outside, and this is the first day of summer break. What the fuck?"

The lights clicked on to find Freddie holding that ice-cold beer to the side of his head and hoping to minimize the ensuing bump he knew was coming. And then Freddie started to laugh when he saw through his bloodshot eyes the blood running down Lee's chin and dripping into an ever growing puddle of red on the floor in front of him. "What the fuck is so funny?" said Lee as he spit out a small piece of tooth along with a mouthful of blood onto Cliff's favorite Lynyrd Skynyrd T-shirt.

"Now that's some funny shit," Freddie said, laughing, as he and Lee high-fived, and Cliff's face turned beet red.

Pop went the tabs on three beer cans. Three best friends, three ice cold beers, and three whole months of summer ahead to down as many of them as they possibly could. That summer would find them inseparable and the beer flowing freely, more so than it ever had before. "Cheers, fellas," said Cliff. "May the good times start now."

It was in Cliff's guest house that they found themselves in. It was a small rectangular house next to the main house where Cliff's mom lived in. He had moved to it from his old bedroom in the main house a few months earlier in the year. It was a small dose of freedom, a place to call his own, and one they had vowed to take full advantage of during that long, hot summer prior to their last year of high school and their last times spent together as three seventeen-year-olds living life to the limits. "Balls to the wall" was how they would say it. It will be a time filled to the brim with alcohol, marijuana, and as many girls as they could possibly slay!

As far as academics went, it was Cliff who ruled the roost. His dad was an orthopedic surgeon and through either a scholarship or his dad's wallet, Cliff had reservations for a college somewhere. His plan was to live it up, party like its 1999, and then dive back into the books, never looking back. It was, in a way, his destiny though he was older than Lee and Freddie by chronological order. He was smaller physically than the other two, not as athletic as his two best friends, but just as competitive and not afraid to mix it up on the b ball court. It was the way most of their evenings were spent. They would be found either on the court up at the farm or in Freddie's dad's drive-way. They loved to drink beer, smoke pot and shoot hoops. The only worries they had in their lives was how long the sun would stay up and the sunlight last so their games could continue.

Cliff swept his arm across the empty cans and beer bottles covering the coffee table and pushed them aside with some of the empty drinks tumbling down onto the floor around their feet. He grabbed his blood-soaked Lynyrd Skynyrd T-shirt from Lee and wiped the tabletop clean of last night's party excesses.

"Here is something special I picked up to get us all hoppin' on this bright and early morning," exclaimed Cliff. As his two friend's watched Cliff reach into the little coin pocket of his Levi's 501 straight-legged jeans.

On to the table, Cliff dropped a small ziplock baggie partially filled with white powdery substance. At first glance, everyone knew right away it was cocaine; nose candy was what they called it. Cocaine had just recently arrived on the scene, and it seemed like it was every-where. "I picked this up a couple of days ago," said Cliff, "knowing you two faggots would be whining about our early morning wake-up call."

It was something they had only done a couple times before, right before an early-morning ski trip they had made to Mt. Hood a few months earlier before spring came rolling into season and that same spring weather was now giving way to the warm summer days

5

waiting just around the corner although, in Oregon, it was sometimes hard to tell what you were going to get from day to day in the way of weather.

"It's just a twenty sack," Cliff said. "Three small lines to jump-start the morning. You guys remember how we talked about going fishin' back during our ski trip?" Cliff asked not really expecting an answer, but instead, he continued on with his narrative. "Well, I am here to inform you that today is that day. So clear your day planners, ladies, because we're going fishin'!"

Although Cliff was just now letting them in on the plan he had known for a week that today would be the day for fishing. In fact, for the past two days, he had been gathering up supplies, readying the gear, and loaded up the old orange-colored pickup truck that was primarily used only for the farm. Cliff's plan was to jump in and go early, knowing that his mother Lisa would be woken up by the truck being started, but she would come up short of doing anything about it before they were down the long graveled driveway and flying down Bishop Road. A clean getaway was what he was looking for.

CHAPTER 2

"Are we at the spot yet? What does the fucking GPS say? Can I get a fucking response, please? Hello? Goddam it! I want some fucking answers, and I want them now!" yelled Colonel North.

There were three men in the back of the boat all dressed like the colonel, who was behind the steering wheel and also the one blurting out all the questions and making all the demands.

All of the men were under orders not to use names especially over the radio headsets. "Yes, sir. We are at the spot now. Keep her steady."

"I'll keep her steady! Let's get that package lowered, secured, and then let's get the fuck out of here!"

"We are moving as fast as we can, sir. Locator beacon set on frequency."

"Tie that fucker off and drop the anchor."

"It's off, sir, and right on the spot. You can get moving anytime, sir."

"It's about time! What took you girls so long?"

"Two bags this time, sir. Remember we had doubled the usual drop. Business is good, you could say."

"Let's get the fuck out of here before we draw any attention."

Four men were on an aluminum-weld jet sled, all wearing black, even covering their faces like ninja warriors. The boat, painted in the same black, was out on the river late at night, dropping two dry bags into the water.

"Draw attention! Where do they find me these clowns?" the colonel wondered.

As quickly as the boat had appeared, it disappeared into the night. One more mission complete. That's one mission for every night that week. Indeed business was good.

CHAPTER 3

Sometimes things go as planned, and their early-morning getaway did. It looked like everything was on their side today. They scrambled out to the barn and finished off the loading of the gear, beer actually, but they thought of it as gear. The only gear that mattered.

"Grab that beer and get it into the coolers," said Cliff.

Lee asked, "Those two older Coleman coolers?"

"No, not these old pieces of shit! Those are my dad's. He thinks they are worth something. Those damn things are too damn heavy. Use the two new Igloo coolers, the plastic ones next to the work bench. Those things are lighter even when they are full of beer. I already have the ice inside them."

After Lee pushed the old classic Coleman coolers back on to the shelf, Freddie and Lee began to load the two Igloo coolers full of beer.

"Do you think forty-eight beers are going to be enough?" Freddie asked with a chuckle.

"I plan on catching a keeper today," answered Cliff. "Even if it takes all day and the only thing we end up catching is a buzz, better to have too many than not enough."

After the beer was all iced down and the coolers loaded, all three jumped into the cab of the 4x4 pickup truck. When everyone was in making sure not to slam the doors, Cliff turned the key.

"Must be our lucky day," yelled Cliff.

The old truck fired up on the very first try. Cliff put it in drive and pulled out of the barn and headed out the driveway just as his mom appeared from out of the front door. "Cliff! Where are you three headed?" asked Lisa.

Cliff and his buddies just waved while the old truck threw up a dust trail. Cliff honked the horn as they headed down Bishop Road.

Their first day of summer break was officially underway. They were off, the radio blasting AC/DCs "Highway to Hell." If they only knew how true that really was.

CHAPTER 4

Not shortly after shedding their all black (ninja-like) outfits, the three men who had earlier dropped their package into the river were summoned into the colonel's office.

"Where in the fuck is my small Pelican case at?" he asked.

"What case are ya talking about, sir?" All three soldiers were standing at attention, but only the highest-ranking soldier was replying.

"How many Pelican cases were there on the boat this morning, ladies?" the Colonel snapped back.

"One, sir!" he replied. "Only one, sir!"

"So then which case do you think I am asking about? Do you have shit for brains son?"

"No, sir"

"So where is my fucking case then, genius?"

"We put it in the dry bags, sir. Before we dropped them in the river, sir!"

"Did I tell you to put the case in the dry bag, you fucking ingrates?" Sounding more and more pissed off by the second and turning redder by the minute.

"You said to put everything into the bags, sir."

"For five years, I have been your superior officer, and over those five years, we have gone on hundreds of missions, both training and real. And over all those missions, not once can I remember you fuck sticks following my orders down to the letter. But now you stand in front of me like Larry, Curly, and Moe, telling me that the one time I need you three stooges to fuck things up, you finally get it right?"

"Well, sir—"

"I'm not asking a question, goddam it. I am stating facts, son, so shut your cocksucker right now and get the fuck out of my office!"

"Yes, si—," the soldier said while starting to salute.

"Now, soldier! Right fucking now, and don't let that door hit you in the ass on your way out!"

With the slamming of the door Colonel North found himself alone in his drab army office, staring at his plain general-issue metal desk, wondering to himself if his long career in the service had just come to a sudden end, if being a general could all but be forgotten, if being a colonel was now only temporary. Lowering himself down into his chair, only stopping for a moment to consider eating his firearm right then and just get it over with. He reached out to his intercom button, wishing he was doing anything else in the world.

"Get the President on the phone, please." It would be the last conversation he would ever have as a colonel, and he knew it more than he had ever known anything at any time in his life. As the phone began to ring in his ear, he once again glanced down at his firearm, wondering just how tasty it might really be.

CHAPTER 5

Reaching the bottom of Bishop Road, the truck made a right-hand turn and headed west down Helvetia Road. "Where the fuck are you going?" asked Lee. "The quickest way to the river is the other way."

Cliff replied, "We are going to a different fishing hole today, fellas. It's a new spot I heard about down at the tavern a few days ago. It's supposed to be a guaranteed fish-catching experience is what I was told by Randy."

Randy was, of course, the owner of the Stumble Inn. It was an old tavern out in the middle of the sticks and most of the customers were regulars, made up of farmers and old country boys. Since it was stuck out in the countryside, Randy would let them come into the bar late at night even though they were still four years away from the legal drinking age. The fact that they regularly hooked Randy up with the best pot around didn't hurt either. In return, Randy let them into the bar to drink, play pool, and drop a little cocaine into their hands from time to time. It was a country tavern for sure, right down to the flannel-shirt, suspender-wearing regulars that filled the stools all along the bar's length. The ceiling was covered with baseball caps from various businesses of the town and local sports teams. The Stumble Inn is home of the best burgers west of the Willamete River and has damn good onion rings too.

They made another right hand turn at Logie Trail and followed it over the hill and headed west along Highway 30.

"That turnoff should be coming up pretty soon," stated Cliff.

"Are you nuts? There ain't no turnoffs around here unless they go down to the old shut-down Trojan Nuclear power plant," Freddie said as he pointed to the abandoned steam stacks, the remains which were left as a reminder of the decommissioned power plant.

"That's exactly where Randy said to go. Supposedly, there is a road between the trees with a broken gate."

Almost as it was being said, Cliff slammed on the brakes, sending smoke off of all four tires and yanking hard to the right on the steering wheel, almost rolling the old 4x4 truck.

"Jesus H Christ," yelled Freddie. "You trying to fucking kill us or what?"

Lee only laughed, partly because it seemed like he was only living life if he was living on the edge of disaster, and partly because Freddie being the smaller of the two got stuck riding bitch (in the middle) and thus was being smashed between the two of them.

"Any closer, Big Boy," Freddie told Lee, using the nickname he liked to call Lee with. "and you will be riding in my lap! And stop spilling your goddamn beer all over me!"

Lee could only laugh again as was common with the guy. He was a big teddy bear of an almost-adult male and a permanent fixture on the varsity football team for the last two years. He was headed toward his final season as a senior for the Glencoe Crimson Tide. Saying he was a big boy was like calling the Columbia River a big creek. He stood 6'2" tall, the youngest of four brothers raised in the family's country home. He was used to being picked on, beat up, and whatever else you want to call it. What it translated into was a man-child who didn't feel pain of any sort and in fact he was only happy when his body was in fifth gear, peddle to the metal with a collision with another body his main focus. A perfect model of a defensive lineman. Rumored to be sought after by several college football teams but interested in none of them. Like every one of the men in his family from Father and every brother he was looking forward to a career in the armed forces. His father and all his brothers were in the Coast Guard. But secretly Lee was thinking of the Navy, another collision no doubt about it only this one would be with his Father.

The road started out pavement, cracked as it was and with weeds and grass growing up in between them. It soon turned into a road which was more weeds and grass than it was pavement until all pavement turned into all weeds with barely a road at all and that road had turned into mostly sand. The truck barreled down the ever diminishing road rounded a corner than popped up over a small hill. Being careful to stay to the right of the Eastern most steam stack as instructed they came to a stop just over the hill and just like it was described to him. All three of them were staring at the mighty Columbia River maybe seven feet in front of them.

"Here it is boys. Sturgeon Point!" exclaimed Cliff.

They all piled out from the cab of the truck and onto the desolate beach. Cliff and Lee laughing as they noticed how much beer Freddie was actually wearing due to the somewhat bumpy ride. Freddie took it in stride as he walked down to the water's edge.

"fuck you both and for laughing you fuckers can unload the gear yourselves!: said Freddie while pulling off his beer soaked shirt and shorts leaving him standing next to the river wearing nothing but his Adidas Sneakers and his Tommy Hilfiger boxer briefs and yelling "you get to ride bitch on the way back Lee!"

The two friends could only laugh and started packing all of the gear down to the river's edge. They also knew that no matter what Freddie would have one reason or another actually an excuse of one or another to not pack any of the gear out of the truck. It would also be the same way when it came time to leave and the gear needed to be packed up so they could be on their way home. These three friends could give you a play by play rundown about which next move either of them would make. That's why they had been and always would be the best of friends. Nothing had ever gotten in between them, but the ultimate test would be coming soon.

CHAPTER 6

"On line 2, sir." Heard a solemn Colonel North come across his intercom. The call he had to make, but the last phone call in all of his life he wanted to make.

"Sir, hello, sir." North said as he answered phone call from the Commander in Chief of the strongest military in the entire free world and also his boss.

"Sir, I….."

"Sir, yes, I ….."

"No, sir."

"Of course, sir, I…"

"Yes, sir, I…"

"Right away, sir. I…" and the phone line at the other side of the United States went dead. North could imagine the handset being slammed down hard enough to break it in two as it crashed upon the cradle, but he knew it was his phone that he was thinking of not the President of the United States phone because he would never show anger of any kind to anyone. He wore the face of a seasoned poker player that had everything on the line or a seasoned actor of the silver screen. Either way you look at it, you could never ever read what next move was to be made by the most powerful man in the world.

Once again pressing down on the intercom button, he barked out, "Would you get my men in here on the double!"

CHAPTER 7

As Cliff and Lee were still unloading the gear, Freddie already had his line in the water, a beer in his hand as he sat in his lawn chair, wearing nothing but his underwear and a smile.

"This is the life!" Freddie exclaimed and then smiled like he was the first to utter those words.

"Fuck you!" replied Lee. "And if you think you're going to pull this shit again and not help load all of this shit back into the truck, you got another thing coming."

Freddie smiled and ignored the words Lee had said. Neither of them believed him, so why pretend? The middle finger of his right hand proclaimed Lee as being number one.

Lee crushed his second beer can before the truck was even unloaded. "Which one of you cocksuckers brought the weed?"

In unison his buddies answered, "I did," and all of them laughed.

"Toss me an empty can Lee and I will get us a pipe all ready to go" Freddie said.

So as the other two got their poles fixed with bait and ready to cast into the river, they were almost ready when Freddie screamed, "FISH ON! FISH ON!"

They were slightly pissed off and at the same time were happy that Freddie was already into the fish. They were pissed because he was always first since he never unloaded anything but his own fishing pole and enough bait for one. They both watched as they drank beer and plotted against their first loaded bowl of weed on this first day of summer break. Freddie fought. They watched and twenty minutes later. He dragged out of the water and onto the beach a fish that was two feet long, a shaker.

"Fuck! Freddie, my dick is bigger than that guppy you fought so hard to drag in," Lee said while laughing.

"Well then, you have a very bright future in the porn movie business," Freddie replied, and they all laughed. "First fish caught, last pitcher bought! I get you two every time!"

Freddie released his shaker while Lee cast out his line and Cliff got ready. "Watch this, you lightweights," yelled Lee. "If you wanna catch anything bigger than my cock, you have to cast it way the fuck out there."

They all watched as his bait flew out and passed Freddie's cast by almost double.

"Good cast, Big Boy!"

Cliff baited up his hook first with a whole fish head then threaded his whole hook through a full unopened can of cat food, which he had already poked several holes in by using a nail and hammer.

"How in the fuck are you going to cast out that load of shit?' Lee asked "and what the fuck is that thing?"

"This is something I borrowed from Randy, and it's also the thing that's gonna bring in the big fish," replied Cliff as he cleared an area of ground up on the small hill and then drove three stakes into the ground. "Now pay close attention. This is how you cast if you wanna catch a fish bigger than Lee's cock!" Cliff exclaimed and Freddie laughed.

"In your face!" Freddie said, pointing his finger at Lee.

"Fuck you both!" was Lee's response. Cliff pulled the arm back on the loaded spring contraption, which had what looked like a bowl attached to it. He set his bait into the bowl, picked up his pole then released the drag, yelling, "Bombs away!" he slammed his foot down on the release and what happened next was a thing of beauty. Cliff's bait was launched, not cast! Launched twice as far or farther than Lee's, it came down with a splash onto the channel of the river.

"That's too far," said Lee.

"He's right" said Freddie.

"Fuck you both," replied Cliff.

"Son of a bitch," They all said and then all together they laughed.

"Load a bowl motherfucker!" Lee shouted.

"Time for a beer and a bowl," Lee continued as he tossed his buddies each a fresh beer, Freddie packed a bowl. They all took up residence side by side in their lawn chairs, perfectly content. If this was all they did all day was to drown a lot of bait and get loaded, they could live with that outcome. Lee delivered another round of beers and then, once again, sat down but not before moving the fullest cooler next to his chair. In silence, the three of them sat drinking and fishing.

As they sat down to smoke a bowl, they noticed that they had no lighter. "Fuck," said Cliff. "Go get a book of matches from the glove box." Freddie retrieved the matches and returned to his lawn chair.

"It doesn't get any better than this!" Cliff said, laughing. "We could do an Old Milwaukie commercial, huh?" he asked then they all laughed.

CHAPTER 8

"Your men are here, sir." squawked the intercom.

"Send them in please," North replied. The three soldiers hurried into the colonel's office and quickly stood at attention in front of his desk.

"You're probably wondering why I've called you ladies together this afternoon," North began.

"Sir, yes, sir." They gave the appropriate response.

"I'm not asking a fucking question, girls, so for the time being, it would be in your best interest to shut your cocksuckers and listen, and listen carefully would be my suggestion. That Pelican case I mentioned earlier was not supposed to go into those bags, ladies. Those belong to the man that signs our paychecks. When informed of the little mishap, his suggestion that it would be in my best interest to get them back. Now I am suggesting to you, three stooges, the very same thing. Shit rolls downhill, ladies, and you, I am afraid are at the bottom of that hill. What you are up against is time, ladies. That package is going to be picked up shortly after dark tonight, and we need to get to it first. All we need is that case back. The rest of it stays put to be picked up tonight. That being said, I am wondering to myself what the fuck you are doing still standing in front of me. Move it, girls, or we will all be on latrine duty before the sun comes up. Again."

CHAPTER 9

"I don't know, Cliff. I think you got it out there too far into the channel," Lee said, and Freddie agreed.

"Give it time," was his reply. "You two aren't late for some important engagement, are you?"

"If you insist, but I am going for new bait," Freddie said as he began to reel in his line. "I've still got the only fish today, losers!" he continued.

"Keep it up, little man, and you will end up in the river yourself," Lee returned and Cliff agreed.

Freddie called Lee, Big Boy, and Lee called Freddie, Little Man. On the basketball court, they called each other Power Move and Sky Walker respectively.

The two friends had been on the same football team for a few years now and ended up in a few of the same classes together. Freddie had met these two friends/country boys in junior high school, and the three had been tight ever since. Freddie would ride his bike the eleven miles between his house and Cliff's almost every weekend, so they could hang out, drink beer, and smoke pot.

Freddie was the city boy who lived with his dad and two brothers in Hillsboro. A natural athlete, he had a place on the varsity squad no matter which sport he was playing. He had lots of friends to hang out with, but these were the chosen two. Ask anybody and they would say he was college sports bound. Possibly get a scholarship, but ask him and he would say, "Majoring in pot smoking and girl chasing." Especially Jenny, she was the one he had his eyes on, but for some reason, he could never get. Not even being a star athlete, a letterman, could he draw the kind of attention from Jenny that he desired.

"Well, it looks like I've been soaking this bait long enough. Maybe you two are actually right for a change, and I should reel this thing in," Cliff said, and his friends didn't disagree.

"Damn, dudes. This thing is fuckin hard to reel in," stated Cliff.

"Come on, sissy girl, pull that thing in," his friends laughingly said.

"I'm trying. It doesn't want to reel."

"Looks like you caught yourself a log," they replied with more laughter.

"Fuck you, guys. Are you going to help me or not?"

For the next half hour, they took turns pulling and reeling and drinking, of course. "Shit! Maybe you got yourself a big one on the line. Fuck! This is a bitch!" cried Lee.

"Should we just cut the line?" asked Freddie as he approached with a knife drawn.

"No!" yelled Cliff. "Don't you dare cut it!" No sooner than he finished those words and his prized catch came to the surface. They all saw it at the same time. There were two of them, and they were yellow. It appeared that one was on top of the other or connected together like Siamese twins. Whatever it, was it looked like it was alien or maybe it was a byproduct of the former nuclear power plant. With one more good pull of the fishing rod and twirl of the reel, it came fully out of the water. Both bodies with that one blinking eye.

"What the fuck!" said by all in unison.

Cliff went first. "Looks like a couple of dry bags and a homing device."

Lee and Freddie said nothing. They only stood there, looking and listening so far. They thought Cliff was doing an excellent job in his description.

Cliff continued, "Let's get 'em pulled all the way out of the water and up by the truck. Lee, you cut off that homing device and show us how far you can throw it out into the river."

Neither questioned his orders. When Cliff began to say things with such confidence, they never questioned him and only did what he asked and immediately.

Splash! Down went the device, homing or otherwise, no one knew for sure. It went about halfway out to where Cliff's bait had gone an hour and a half earlier. At the same moment, Freddie cut loose the dry bags and began to pull open one of the Velcro-fastened ends.

"Jesus H. Christ!" Freddie screamed while staring in to the opening he had just created.

"What? What did you find?" Cliff asked.

Freddie reached into the bag, grabbed a handful then held it up for him to see.

"A whole bunch of these!"

Neither one of them said a word. They only stood there wide eyed and staring. No words would come out, only their mouths falling open for what seemed like an eternity.

"Put them back into the bag now!" ordered Cliff. "Put them back into the bag now," he said a second time. "Now throw them both into the back of the truck. Forget everything else. Let's get them into the back of the truck and then let's get the fuck out of here now!"

With quickness, Freddie threw them in to the back of the truck while Cliff jumped into the cab and fired it up. Lee was already climbing in when Freddie jumped in the back and yelled. "I'm gonna ride back here and make sure nothing happens to them," he said, smiling from ear to ear.

CHAPTER 10

The jet sled was being pushed to its limits as the three soldiers bounded their way up the river. They were not dressed like the ninjas of the night before but were still leery of being seen taking care of the business at hand while hoping to get in and get out before anyone showed up ready to scoop up their prize. A look of horror came over their faces as they came around the bend. Their eyes had been captured by the bright yellow rope that had been pulled up onto the sand. Behind it was an anchor with the letters USA painted on it.

They spent little time investigating the beach campsite. It didn't take long to find the only clue that was left behind, a single matchbook with the name The Stumble Inn printed in red on top of its white face. The threesome snapped a few photos of the campsite and then they shoved off from the beach. They spent the whole ride back to the base, knowing the severity of the news they had for Colonel North, and secretly, all three thought it might be best to turn the boat into the opposite direction, get off at some secluded area, and try to disappear into the world. It would not happen because they all knew there was no hiding, no hiding at all, anywhere, not from this. It would never be allowed. They would be found; it was only a matter of time.

As night fall crept in and started taking over its hold on the day, their only thoughts were how many toilets would they have to clean before retirement blessed the ending of their careers.

CHAPTER 11

Cliff drove like a man possessed until he reached the main road, Highway 30, realizing that getting pulled over and asked a bunch of questions, some he could answer and some he could not, all of it could only turn bad. So he drove the speed limit and watched his mirrors nervously, saying nothing.

"Is someone going to answer my fuckin question or what?" Lee was now yelling for the third time. "What's in the fucking bags?"

This snapped Cliff back out of his trance long enough to motion him to slide open the rear window and say, "Ask Freddie. I am too busy driving."

Lee found this odd for Cliff was always doing seven things at once while he was driving, usually being oblivious to what the traffic was doing. Lee slid open the rear window.

"What the fuck has gotten into Cliff? Why in the fuck did we leave all that beer back there? Did you remember to grab that weed off the log?" questioned Lee.

Not knowing which order to answer the big guy's questions, all Freddie could do is reach down into the dry bag and pull out a handful to show him, the same way he had done for Cliff.

"Both bags?" Lee asked.

Freddie nodded instead of speaking. He was still a few moments away from breaking away from his speechless state of mind that he had so suddenly been shocked into.

"How much do you think is there?" asked Lee, who now had more questions than answers. At least more than he had before Freddie's little display.

Freddy was finally able to muster one single word as he stuffed the bundled stacks of one hundred dollar bills back into the bags. "Millions!"

The rest of the way home, Cliff drove as careful as a kid on his first driving lesson with Dad by his side. Next to him, Lee had turned into the biggest back eat driver the world had ever seen, and Freddie lay across the top of those dry bags, keeping them from flying out of the truck. All three of them were smiling from ear to ear while all at the same time thinking, "This is going to be the best summer break ever!"

CHAPTER 12

As the summer sun settled into the western horizon and night fall swiftly took its place until morning, the three soldiers all with sullen faces stood in front of their colonel's desk all at attention, saying nothing, and for all intent and purposes, nothing needed to be said. Three staring at one, and one staring at three and all thinking that the summer sun was all to symbolic in as much as their careers were a dying light and blackness would now over take it.

The colonel could only scratch his head first, looking at the digital photos taken earlier then at his phone on his desk then back again, knowing what call he was going to have to make and wishing he was anywhere but in the here and now.

"Dismissed," North said half heatedly, a faint nod of his head and wave of his hand.

Holding the intercom button down. "Would you please get the President on the line?"

Now his glances were in a circle of three photos, phone and service revolver. And again and again.

North was not stupid by any means. He knew from the beginning all too clearly his position in this little/big scheme was. The word "scapegoat" had crossed his mind more and more as this most recent mission continued. It was a position he was very familiar with, but he knew that only failure could make him that scapegoat, and for the first time in his career, he could taste failure on the tip of his tongue and smell it with every inhaling breath he took. Photos, phone, service revolver. He knew he would never eat his gun, no matter how tasty it looked to him. North bled red, white, and blue down to his very soul and that's why he was the chosen one, and that why he knew it was time for him to take one for the team, and that's why he would do a stellar job, filling that role, serving his country.

The phone rang, startling him out of his deep thoughts.

"Hello, sir."

"Someone got the bags, sir, the baby has been lost."

"Yes, sir."

"Yes, sir."

"Good-bye, sir."

Their conversations had grown way too one sided in recent days, North thought as he set his phone back down into its waiting cradle. Pressing the intercom button down, he said, "Please rally my men and have them meet me at the Hummer. We will be picking up some guests at the airport around midnight."

"Yes, sir, right away," his secretary replied.

CHAPTER 13

The orange 4x4 truck rolled onto the gravel driveway that it had left behind this morning as the evening sky filled with bright brilliant shades of yellow, orange, red, and colors that had no names. Sunsets were one of the many reasons Cliffs parents had purchased these forty acres of prime Helvetia farm land/forest not so many years ago. Since then, a separation had taken place between his mom and dad, leaving Cliff at this hilltop island with his little sister, His younger brother spent most of his time with his dad at the Doctors West Hills bachelor's pad. There was the main farmhouse from whose decks, you could overlook the entire city of Hillsboro and far beyond from east to south and all the way west. A tall stand of Oregon forest blocked any view to the north, and in front of those woods is where the one-hundred-year-old barn sat, in between the house and the barn. Slightly west stood the farm's guesthouse and its most recent inhabitant, Cliff, more specifically, Cliff and his closest friends had the house all to themselves as well as the forty acres of farm fields and forest, including the barn, their teenage wonderland. On top of the hill, they could and would do whatever they chose to do without any interference from any outsiders. It was here that they all felt safe to explore and led adventurous lives that only the teenage mind could conjure up. And when it came down to it, these three had become champions at mischief.

"Cliff, where in the hell have you been all day?" Lisa asked while storming into the barn, nearly catching the three of them stashing the two yellow dry bags full of cash under the hay bales. "You know I use the truck on Saturdays! You didn't even ask if you could take it at all let alone all day long!"

All three of them cringed when they heard Lisa swear. She did not swear often, but when she did, they knew they all had some explaining to do and that yard work was going to be part of their very near future.

"Shit, Mom!" Cliff quickly came back. "It's the first day of summer break, and we wanted to go fishin', and we didn't want to hear you say no!"

"Well you messed up my plans for the day, and that's not a very good way to start summer break. Did you catch anything?"

"Freddie pulled in a shaker, so yes, we caught something, but nothing we could keep."

"It looks to me like you lost a whole bunch of gear, and it better not be my new Igloo coolers that are missing!" Lisa shot back, giving them a look that said she wasn't buying the whole story. "You three need to tighten up your game. I smell something fishy, and we know it ain't fish," Lisa finished her sentence with a smile. Letting them all know that she had her eye on them and reminded them that they had fallen short of trying to get one by her every time in the past, and that this would be no different.

`"That was fucking close!" chimed Freddie, but only after seeing Lisa enter the house some yards away. "So how are we gonna get these down to the guesthouse without your mom seeing?" continued Freddie.

"Here's the plan," started Cliff. "We really only need one of them for the moment since we can assume that they both are packed the same way, so while Freddie and me go to my mom's house to grab some food, Lee can carry one around the back of the barn and sneak it over to the side deck of the guest house."

"Why me? Why do I have to wade through all of the cow shit?" asked Lee.

"Because those fuckin bags are heavy," replied Cliff." And that my friend is a good thing." He was smiling as he finished his sentence. "Besides, I'll buy you a new pair of shoes myself," Cliff said laughing as he and Freddie headed out the barn door. "Watch out for the goat." He laughed then elbowed Freddie then they both laughed.

As they walked to the main house, Freddie served up the questions while Cliff volleyed back the answers or at least what would have to serve as answers for the moment.

"Do you think that both bags are really stuffed full of hundred dollar bills?"

"Yes, you saw better than both of us what are in those bags, and you said millions."

"Do you think that is a good estimate?"

"Yes I do, million with an S at the end."

"What do you think we have stumbled into?"

"That, my friend, has got to be the million-dollar question."

"Yeah, I suppose you are right."

"Yeah, I suppose I am."

"Do you think…," Freddie started to asked and then paused long enough that Cliff jumped into finish his sentence.

"Yes, Freddie. Trouble could be a distinct possibility! I think we can do things to keep it at bay. At least I think we can."

"I am starving. You starving? I know Lee is always starving!"

Cliff turned and grabbed Freddie by the shoulders. "Listen Freddie," Cliff said. "If we run into my mom and she starts asking questions, I want you to keep your pie hole shut! Everyone knows you turn into babbling idiot."

"Jesus Christ, Cliff, you don't have to be such a dick about it," Freddie shot back.

"Yes, I do," said Cliff. "If you start talking, you won't shut up until my mom knows your whole fucking life story. You let me handle my mom! If she starts asking you questions, say you have to take a piss and go outside. She's already on to us and I don't need you blowing it."

With that, they stepped inside his mom's house at the same time Lee stepped around the barn, dodging the goat and lifting, barely, the dry bag onto the guest house deck.

CHAPTER 14

Out on the river, the night-time darkness and silence was broken in sentences both in English and Spanish as they navigated their boat toward Sturgeon Point and also toward their waiting package. They had made this trip before and, recently, more and more frequently, and this made them and, more importantly, the men's boss very happy, and their boss was the kind of man you most certainly didn't want to upset, let alone make angry.

"Turn right," yelled one of the men.

"The signal is getting stronger to the right."

One man steered the boat, one monitored the homing device locator, and one man readied himself by pulling on his wet suit and dawning his air tanks.

"Okay, okay, right here. Steady the boat right here.

The frogman lowered himself slowly into the water, stuck in his mouthpiece, and then disappeared into the water's blackness. A few moments later, he resurfaced with the homing device in hand and nothing else. They all looked from one to the other and back again, each searching for the answers that would not come.

Looking at each other meant no one else was watching where the boat was drifting toward. Then all of the sudden, the frogman could touch bottom, and soon after that, the bottom of the boat scraped against something. One man grabbed for a search light to see how bad it was and when that light fanned across the shoreline the answers to their questions were beginning to come clear.

They eased the bow of the boat up onto the shoreline, and then they strolled toward the little abandoned campsite. One man opened the cooler next to the lawn chair, reached in, and pulled out an ice-cold beer, popped the top, and took a long pull off of it. Another man reached down and picked up the white matchbook and the bag of weed, putting them both into his shirt breast pocket. All of them boarded the boat along with the cooler full of ice-cold beer.

In silence, they glided their boat back to their docking slip, downing several beers along the way. Once they were back into their hotel room, one of them men called their boss. The other took a long drag off the pipe.

Instructions on how to proceed would be coming soon, and if the past was any indication of how it was going to be, they would deliver them swiftly and assuredly.

CHAPTER 15

The small Lear jet touched down with very few eyes noticing. It taxied to the small hangar at the far side of the Hillsboro Airport. Everyone figured this would have a better chance at not causing any commotion and for all intents and purposes they had figured it right.

The airplane doors with stairs attached swung open to the ground, and the next moment, two men looking every bit the part of the Secret Service, CIA, FBI, or any other top secret United States agency stepped from the aircraft and walked to the waiting military Hummer.

As they sat down in the backseat of the Hummer, they found North riding shotgun, and the driver was some peon, probably under North's command. Once their bags were loaded, the hummer rolled out of the airport's back gate, turned right onto Brookwood Parkway and headed south toward the Holiday Inn Express where the two men had adjoining rooms waiting for them.

They grabbed their bags from the back of the Hummer, set them on the ground, and then just before they turned to walk toward the hotel, one man stopped and said, "Thanks for the ride. Here's your tip. Now from this moment on, we suggest that you and your grade A, bona fide fuckups stay clear, and let us, the professionals, mop up this fuckin' mess you made! Do I make myself clear?" the man asked North and studied his face, waiting for his reply.

North's only response was to raise the middle fingers of both his hands. North's driver then let the Hummer roll back a few feet then stepped on the gas pedal, let the clutch fly, running over one of the men's duffle bag luggage, shooting it out from under the Hummers rear tire.

North slapped his knee and laughed out loud. "That was stellar, son."

That was all North would say the rest of the way back to his headquarters. A very small grin rested upon his face, and you could never tell he was thinking that in some ways, the guy was right. They did fuck things up. North also knew he would be raked over the coals before this mess ran its coarse and this mess became an afterthought to the American public. The same way everything did. North also knew taking one for the team would also fade from memory fast. Deep down, he hoped that those two would fuck things up bigger than he and his men did. The smile, subtle as it was, returned to North's face.

CHAPTER 16

"What the fuck took you fuckers so fucking long?" asked Lee as Cliff and Freddie entered the guest house. "And what the fuck is up with that goat? He chased me all the way around the barn and tried to bite me when I was going over the fence! I had to hit him with one of the dry bags! That fucking goat is mean!"

"This did, you fuckin faggot!" Freddie said smiling and handed him a whole pizza. Anything less, and he would find the big guy taking food off his plate too.

Cliff answered the big guy's questions next. "Ever since that goat got into last year's marijuana patch and ate every one of my plants right down to the ground, he has been fucking crazy and mean as hell. I told you to watch out for him." Cliff finished with a laugh, rubbing his palms together. Cliff asked, "Where are that bags, Lee?"

"Right here motherfucker!" Lee said as he stood up and lifted one end of the couch up. I wanted it right where I knew no one could get to it. In fact, here is the other one too," he said as he lifted Cliffs chair. "I just couldn't leave it out there in the barn all by itself."

Lee re-lifted furniture while Freddie pulled them out one by one. "Fuck these things are a lot heavier than I remember. Must have been running on adrenaline."

"Okay," Cliff started, "here is the deal. Whatever we get out of these bags we split three ways equally. No bitchin or complaining. I don't think that's going to be a problem since, technically, it was my line that caught them."

Both his friends only nodded, not interrupting Cliff. They both knew this was coming, that Cliff would have a plan, for he always had the wheels inside his head turning. They could make suggestions, but they knew this was going to be the plan. That Cliff had been thinking up this plan from the moment they found the bags; in fact, they were counting on it.

"After we split it, we will only take a small amount. A small equal amount that we all agree on. The rest of it goes into hiding for the time being. We need to not draw attention to ourselves, right, Lee?"

"Yes!" Lee replied. "Why do you say that only to me?'

"Well, let's see," Cliff said. "Remember the time you were supposed to hold the lighter and you set the flag pole on fire? I could mention many more instances, if you would like me to continue answering your question."

"Man, you guys never let a guy forget." Lee laughed a little bit inside and wore a tiny smile on his face to prove it.

"Look, guys, I am not fucking around here!" Cliff continued. "I know you both have thought about it already. We have stumbled upon something that somebody is going to start missing at some point in time. Somebody put it there, so somebody will be coming back to get it, and that's assuming it wasn't left for anyone else. If that is the case, then there will be two people who will be missing it. I figured, if whoever it is has this kind of money, they have plenty more to do—a thorough investigation in order to find it and recover it. They are going to want it back. We take a little, and we bury the rest and wait awhile until things cool down, so to speak."

"How long is that?" Lee enquired.

"As long as it fuckin' takes!" squawked Freddie. "Jesus H. Christ, Lee! You were a broke dick when we woke up this morning, now you are probably a fucking millionaire. Do you want to fuck up and lose it all and go back to being that same broke dick? That's why he singled you out, fuck!"

"Come on, guys. Let's not let this get in between us. There is plenty for all if we play our cards right. There is no one but us that know we have it, and there is no way for anybody to start thinking we have it. Now we agree to do this and to do it right, and if we do, we are set for life. So let's shake on it many times, and then burn a bowl on it, and then we can get down to the counting part. I don't know about you, but that sounds like fun to me!"

So they shook on it, smoked a bowl, and then got ready to count.

"Check it out. I am going to lock the doors and pull the curtains. No one enters until it's all counted. We will take a small share, and then it's all put away, ready for hiding. No discussions, no objections!" Cliff finished, and no objections followed.

Fresh beers were passed out, and the first bag was un-Velcroed and then dumped out on top of the huge coffee table, which was made from an old ship's cabin door. There was enough to cover it and part of the floor around it.

"Let's put it into stacks of ten and rows of ten and then we can add the rows of ten together time one hundred thousand" Cliff suggested. The numbers sounding ridiculous as they rolled off his tongue and it sounded just as unreal when landing on their ears.

So they started building stacks and rows of 10 x 10, which equals a million dollars per row. Along they went, building stack after stack after stack. When the coffee table began to vanish under the cover of hundred dollar bills, the stacking was complete. Before them sat stacks of 10 x 10.

"Fifteen million bucks!" exclaimed Cliff. "So far that comes to five million each, so I am guessing we can double that by two and say we have ten million dollars each. Not a bad day of fishing, boys!"

They sat there speechless. In front of them lay more money than they could have ever imagined. They thought to themselves what they would buy and the phrase "not a bad day of fishing, boys!" echoed, and they liked it.

That's one down and one to go. They needed to count it that night as per their deal. That Cliff had been very clear on, and they would stick to the plan.

Lee un-Velcroed the second dry bag and poured it out on the coffee table. From inside the big bag, a small case tumbled out onto the table. That was something unexpected and startled them all.

"Holy shit!" said Lee "What do you make of that!"

"My best guess is that it is a small Pelican case. If we are going by what it says on the front of it," Cliff replied.

"Okay, smartass! Are you going to open it or am I?"

Before he could finish, Freddie had the case open and was holding two discs in his hand and saying, "This is it. Nothing else."

The discs were returned to the case, and the money counting continued. As expected, the bag held another fifteen million dollars. Yes, indeed, they all had become instant millionaire's time ten. All three sat there staring at the big pile of money. The second one they had seen that day.

"I need a bong hit!" Freddie cried out. "And I think I will chase it down with a beer!"

Both of his friends agreed that they should have one as well.

Cliff spoke first. "Let's put it all back in the bag and hold out, one banded stack of hundreds each. That's ten thousand each. In my opinion, that is too much, but that's how much I want."

"Sounds good to me," said Freddie.

"Me too," Lee said.

"As far as these discs go, I say we take a trip into town later today and visit Frank. He will be able to tell us what's on them. I also say, let's have a beer in celebration and take an oath that we tell no one. Not a soul."

To this they all agreed they also agreed that counting that much money was hard work and that a trip to the main house for more pizza would be a good idea. They ate, drank, smoked, and did not sleep. Try as they may, sleep would not come.

CHAPTER 17

As one satellite phone was dialed from Portland, Oregon, another one ran deep in the jungles of South America. It was the personal phone of Pablo Escobar, kingpin of the South American drug trade. As Pablo listened, he was told how his men had found Pablo's money was not recovered! Pablo was told about the drop zone and the left-over campsite they had encountered on the sandy beach as well as the matchbook with the name of the Stumble Inn on it. Abandoned coolers full of beer, fishing poles thrown away in haste, not to mention a beer can that had been converted into a pot pipe with its bowl loaded and ready to be smoked. "With very good pot in it," the man had added. When the man had finished with his detailed report, he was instructed to stand by the phone until further instructions could be given.

Pablo leaned back in his chair after hanging up the phone, kicked his feet up on his massive hand-carved wooden desk that had absolutely nothing on it. He closed his eyes and rubbed at his temples and sat there in contemplation, trying to figure out what his next move should be. Surely, outsiders had stumbled upon the loot accidently. Too many odd clues for it to be any other way. Besides, the figureheads in place in the US government would never cross him in such a way or would they? They certainly had no problems sneaking behind their citizens' back to enter into the cocaine business with him. What he knew for sure was that he would have no choice other than to send his men in to find out what happened to his thirty million dollars. It could not, it would not, go by with nothing happening. And when he did respond, it would be certain that everyone knew it was him who had sent down the orders. Someone was going to pay for this, that much was a guarantee.

The three men sat in their hotel room overlooking downtown Portland and across the Willamette River. All of them were cleaning their guns. They would be called into action soon, and they had better be ready when the order came down for they knew that their boss had a way of getting what he wanted.

CHAPTER 18

As morning dawned their sleepless night the three of them, still sitting with the curtain drawn, door locked. A temporary prison they had created for themselves although this was a prison to keep others out not hold then in. The guest house, as they called it, was a small rectangle of a building. Within it were one bedroom, one bathroom, a kitchen, and a front room. Though it wasn't very large, there was plenty of room for a high school kid to live in and plenty of room for his friends to party with him. Over Cliff's short stay, the three of them had certainly proved that the house contained within its belly all the things they needed: a fridge to fill with beer, the sink provided water for their bong. and the woodstove provided heat.

All three of them sat silently like they had most of night, staring at those dry bags full of a teenager's wildest dreams and flipping through their ten thousand dollar down payments. More spending money than any of them had ever had or ever thought of having.

"Here's what I think we should do," said Cliff, breaking the latest bout of silence the boys were experiencing. "We take the bags minus the discs and thirty thousand dollars and bury them up in the hay loft. If we put them toward the back corner, it will be next year before anybody would get to them. After that we take a ride into town and buy Lee that new pair of shoes and maybe get us a pair or two as well. It will also give us a chance to break some of these hundreds so it doesn't draw any attention."

"Fuck yea! I'm gonna buy me a pair of Adidas Superstars in every color stripes they have!" exclaimed Freddie.

"Maybe we should exercise a little bit more self-control than that," replied Cliff. With the plan in place, they settled back, passed the bong around until they finished their morning beers. They loaded up and headed to the barn.

It took them close to an hour to bury the bags deep in the hay loft as well as fill the troughs with hay, making it look to his mom that Cliff had just done his chores. If she had been watching. Next they were hopping into Cliff's 1980 Datsun 200sx his dad had bought him for his sixteenth birthday. They referred to it as the Red Racer. Silently, they all thought an upgrade was needed and wondered how long they could wait until they made that move.

Three teenage boys all with ten thousand dollars trying to burn holes in their pockets. Indeed, how long could they wait? They made a beeline for the sports stores at Washington Square. They all figured they were going to answer that question very soon. Had they been pressed for an answer they would have said fifteen minutes. Cliff hit the power button on his tape deck and the radio played "Bad to the Bone" by George Thorogood. They turned it up as loud as they could.

CHAPTER 19

They descended upon the mall, Washington Square. Like men on a mission, no sports store selling shoes was going to be safe or ignored. They started at one end of the largest shopping mall in the Portland Metro or Tri-County area, and it was filled with such stores as Nordstrom, Macy's, JC Penny, and Sears; a multitude of jewelry stores as well as small store fronts specializing in high-end electronics; and a food court that the three friends would not neglect before they were finished with their urban assault, packing plenty of ammunition. Their focus that day, however, was sports stores. The kind that had shoe displays from floor to ceiling and running from store front all the way to the back. Stores with names like Foot Locker, the Athlete's Foot, Coaches, and their most favorite one named, Three Stripe Sports. There they specialized in nothing but the latest and greatest, most recent releases and original Adidas shoes. They found it odd now that they could afford to buy out the whole store if they had chosen to do so, but they now seemed to have their sights more on the item they wanted compared to in the past, which was items they could only afford.

They entered Three Stipe Sports with eyes as wide as saucers and drooling at the mouth. Neither one of them had yet broken a one hundred dollar bill, but they all sensed that this was about to change. Stripes of every color grabbed their attention, especially the selection of Superstar basketball shoes and the latest model to hit the shelves called Top Tens high tops and low cut models in all colors.

Freddie finished his shopping first, and the clerk bagged up two pairs of Superstars with green stripes and black stripes, one pair of low-cut Top Tens with blue stripes, and two pairs of Superstar sweat-pants both black with white stripes. It was his favorite sweatpants, and he wanted to buy them all. As he peeled off four bills to cover his $349 total, he leaned into the clerk, handed him another thousand dollars to him and said that it was to cover his friends tab, "Keep the rest for yourself," Freddie finished. The clerk ended his shift with a three-hundred-dollar tip. The clerk followed them out into the mall and watched them leave, yelling, "Come again".

Lee and Cliff fought over who would cover the food tab. Fights like these they planned on having for the rest of their lives. You could even say hoped for. They split the bill and headed back toward Hillsboro. They had to make a trip to see their computer geek friend Frank, and they knew he would love the brand new, top-of-the line computer disc reader/writer they had picked up for him at the mall.

CHAPTER 20

Frank lived with his parents but had an entrance into his basement room separate from the house itself. The concrete steps, twenty in all, descended into the ground, and at the bottom was Frank closed but unlocked door. It was always this way. Frank never had too many guests come by to visit his underground bunker filled with whirling sounds as fans turned and intermittent blinking LED lights of red and green gave it the look of something out of a Stephen King novel. As far as looks go, you could also say that Frank had a sci-fi look to him. Leaving his room of solitude only to go to school, which rumors, if to be believed, he didn't have to attend for he got all As and his scholarship would be to whichever college he desired. Frank's skin was colored or uncolored a pale shade of white bordering on what could be described as opaque or even clear as Cliff once suggested but with a following laugh. Frank was a computer geek before there were computer geeks, and the one they knew for sure could show them what was on those discs.

"What's up, my man?" Said Lee.

"Not much," answered Frank. He hated that greeting for he knew he was not their man, at least not until they wanted something from him. "Worried about not having the grades to play football again this year?" Frank shot back. His canned "not much" response he always used because if he tried to explain what was truly up to, no one would understand.

"Stay tuned on that one, Frank. I may need some help in biology this year," Lee said.

"Why would this year's biology be any different than all the years before?" Frank smiled.

"Here you go, smartass. We brought you something we think you will like."

"So the truth is out. You guys want something."

"Frank," Cliff began, "we came across these the other day, and you are the only one we know that might be able to get a look at what's on them." Cliff knew that as soon as the word crossed his lips, nothing would stop Frank from getting to the bottom of those discs. It was a trick they had used on him in the past without fail.

"You know what pisses me off about you guys?" Frank asked in response. "You think you're so smooth, using words like 'might' as a shot at me to prove to you I can. All you have to do is ask there is no need for the tricks!"

Cliff wondered to himself how long had Frank been onto this trick.

"The very first time you used it," Frank said looking directly into Cliff's eyes.

Frank could tell by the look on Cliff's face that he had indeed guessed right. He loved doing that to people. He loved to creep them out. "I'm into reading minds now," he said as he opened the first bag Lee had given to him.

"What the fuck? No fucking way! You know how spendy these things are?"

In fact they did know how much the cost because they all went in on it together once they saw the price tag of $1,500 on the box. Freddie had even asked the store clerk if it was miss-tagged when they took it up to the checkout counter.

"This is the exact one I had my eye on. When connected with my system, I can generate standalone on the fly copies in just minutes."

"That's what the store clerk told us too, so why don't you bust us out two copies real quick then you can call us at Freddie's when you open up the Computer Disc for a look-see. "I'm telling you right now, they are probably with a password or what do they call it?"

Frank cut off Cliff. "Encrypted?" he suggested.

We had him excited now. "Where did you say you got them?"

"I didn't. How about you tell us? It sounds like more fun that way," Cliff responded, knowing they could never tell him the truth.

"Okay, I accept that challenge."

Twenty minutes later, they were back on the road again with the original Computer Discs plus a copy, leaving Frank a copy to try and dig into.

"Do you think Frank can get into them?" Freddie asked.

"Do you know anybody else we can ask?" Cliff replied.

"I'm not doubting the choice. I know of no one else who even has a shot at getting into them. Do you think it's fair not to tell him where they came from?"

"I thought about telling him that we fished them out of the Columbia River while we were fishing yesterday, but I didn't think he would buy that story. Hell, I could have added that we pulled out thirty million dollars as well. Do you think that might have sold him on the story?"

"I see your point. I guess it doesn't matter who we try to sell that story to, does it? Even the President to the United States of America would call us a bunch of liars, huh?"

Little did they know that. He was the only man who would believe that kind of story and then he would probably ask for his disks back.

"While were over this way, we should take a spin by Jenny's and see what she is up to," Freddie suggested.

"Nothing she wants you to know about." Lee laughed.

"Why you gotta be like that? I've got ten million reasons why she might like me now."

"Yeah, but zero you can tell her about."

"Fuck! Why's it gotta be like that?"

"You know why! Don't go fuckin' off our agreement over, pussy!"

Freddie stared out the car's rear window, saying nothing. He knew Cliff and Lee were right, but he also knew that he didn't have to like it.

CHAPTER 21

They did drive by Jenny's house as Freddie had requested but the car didn't stop like he had wanted to. Cliff would not stop for fearing of Freddie flashing his wad, throwing money around and then being coaxed out of every bit of information he had just recently sworn in oath to not tell a soul.

Jenny was a classmate of theirs and had been since the seventh grade. Five years of school with her, and Freddie had been smitten with her since the very first day. The crush had survived five years of rejections of one sort or another, and Cliff guessed it would go on for another five or more years or as long as Freddie was still alive.

There was very good reasons for a crush to exists. Jenny was blonde (naturally, of course, that had never been confirmed, but not for the lack of trying). She had a beautiful smile full of bright white teeth. She had long legs (Freddie would describe them as going all the way up to his face) and a set of bright steely blue eyes. They looked like pools of blue water with sparkles of light flashing in them, and they were way too easy to get lost into. In junior high, she had been a cheerleader, and Freddie had been a star athlete. You would think they were destined to be a couple. However, it was not to be. Their relationship as friends had started so innocently with Freddie walking her home from school in the seventh grade. Jenny's house was on the way to Freddie's, and he would walk with her. Sometimes he would carry her books, and it's a sure bet, if she would have asked, he would have carried her too. Freddie knew how to make her laugh, and he loved to hear that laugh. But like other girls he had chased while she chased other guys, he made her laugh too much. By the time he got up the balls to ask her out, they were too good of friends to be in a serious relationship, so the crush or desire to be her steady boyfriend would continue, but most of it, Freddie kept to himself though his best friends knew how deep his crush ran like nobody else did. Lately, for the most part, Freddie had conceded the fact that what they had was what they had, and that's all it would ever be. Down in his heart, Freddie knew that even if he did come up with ten million reasons for her to change her mind, she wouldn't, and he would be okay with that. He knew that for Jenny, boyfriends of one sort or the other would come and they would go, but he would always be her friend; and to him, that meant everything. The last thing he would ever want is for a relationship to get between them and make things complicated and leave him stripped of everything he hoped for. As long as he had her in his life, he also had hope, and hope was good. Beauty and brains, all in one package, indeed. Hope was good!

CHAPTER 22

While they were passing through town, they decided to stop by and make a showing at Freddie's dad's house. One, to make sure his dad and brothers knew he was okay and to tell them where he was at; second, to drop off some of Freddie's packages; and of course, three, to play some hoops in the driveway.

Freddie's dad's house was a favorite place of theirs to hang out in when they found themselves in town. The house was a big three-level building located in the north side of town, only a couple of blocks from the town's football stadium, Hare Field. On Friday nights, Cliff could park at Freddie's and then would walk over to the game. Parking in the area on game nights was always a pain in the ass. Freddie's dad's house was basically a bachelor pad with four males living there ever since the split-up of his parents a few years ago. The big screen TV was in the front room and always had the latest pay-per-view events showing whatever it be—heavy-weight boxing, so they could see Mike Tyson and his latest victim (that was until Buster Douglas pulled off the upset of the century) or that year's WrestleMania, featuring Hulk Hogan, Randy "Macho Man" Savage, or the Ultimate Warrior (they had never missed a single one), or Monday night football which was always a favorite to light the screen on the 60 inch television. The downstairs was riddled with toys for boys, the centerpiece was a blue-felted pool table, and surrounding it was a pinball machine on one end and a killer stereo system at the other. An all-time favorite was the small fridge that always held a full keg of beer. It was in this room they would gather for pool sessions that might last all night or all weekend, long building a hangover that would most certainly follow them to school come Monday morning. There had been more than one occasion where they would have to sleep it off in the nurse's office during the first couple of periods and then bounce back to finish off the round of afternoon classes that followed lunch break.

That day's mission included nothing more than a bong session in Freddie's room, followed by some b ball in the driveway. The hoop and backboard had been lowered to around 8½ feet so that they were able to pull off the slam dunk moves of their favorite NBA players such as Dominique Wilkins a.k.a. the Human Highlight Film, Darrell Dawkins a.k.a. Chocolate Thunder, Julius Erving a.k.a. Dr. J, and the most recent Portland Trail Blazer's superstar Billy Ray Bates. On most occasions, the game would abruptly end with Lee showing off his latest Chocolate Thunder dunk and ripping the rim down along with a chunk of fiberglass background. That night's game would undoubtedly end the very same way. So once they were primed and all ready to play, they laced up their new Adidas and headed outside to try them out on their very own concrete playground.

"Lob me an alley-oop pass, Cliffy. I'll show you how it's done," yelled Lee.

"Easy, Big Boy. We would all like to stuff a few before you tear the rim down," Cliff shot back.

"Yeah, my dad will be pissed. He just bought this one last week," Freddie stated. "Don't fret about it. I am pretty sure, he won't have to buy the next one." At that remark, they all laughed.

"True," Freddie said and then yelled, "You break it, you buy it."

So the three of them took turns showing their moves and pulling off a various array of slam dunk moves. The afternoon heat was getting to them, and then it came as it usually did and always would. Lee launched himself about ten feet from the basket and power slammed down a two-handed dunk while shouting, "Chocolate Thunder!" He ripped the rim down along with half of the backboard.

Laughing, Lee exclaimed, "I know, I know. You break it, you buy it. Tell you what, I will buy you two of them." He walked around to the side of the garage where the garbage can was stored and tossed the mangled rim onto the small pile of rims that was getting bigger game by game. "It looks like there's six of 'em back there now," Lee said as he returned from around the garage's side.

"I think all but one of those were ones that you ripped down," Freddie replied, smiling because he knew the other one was his doings. "I still remember that flying Dr. J slam I did around the rim when I busted the backboard. It's fun to do."

Freddie and Lee laughed and then slapped a high five.

"I'll close the garage door, leave a note for my dad, and then we can book out of here," Freddie was saying as the garage door started to lower.

When Freddie came back out of the house a few minutes later, he saw the neighbor from across the street talking with Cliff and Lee. And as Freddie approached, his neighbor walked away from them and went back to his house.

"What did the neighbor want?" Freddie asked, but reluctantly. He could tell by the looks on their faces what their answer would be.

"I have no fucking idea!" Cliff said, and Lee made circles around his ear with his finger, saying, "Coo-coo, coo-coo!"

"I already know that part, but what did he say?" Freddie asked again.

"Something to the effect of 'they are watching. Beware and be careful,'" Cliff replied.

"Watching what?"

"That's what we asked."

"And..."

"And then you walked out, and he turned and walked away, never even looking back. That's pretty strange, don't you think?"

"Let's get in the car and get moving and then I will answer that question," Freddie responded.

"So check this out. You already know that we refer to my neighbor as Crazy Harry, right?" Not really asking a question, Freddie continued, "Not to his face, of course, but to each other" (referring to his family). "Well. last week my brothers and I stood in the driveway and watched him try to take the canopy off of his pickup truck using a splitting maul." It was really bad. The cops showed up to stop him and he started yelling at them, telling them to get off of his property. After several minutes of this, they left saying that he wasn't hurting anyone so there was nothing they could do.

Cliff and Lee just looked at each other. "And not too long ago, I was looking out of the kitchen window and saw the PGE (Portland General Electric) meter reader come walking out from the side of his house, holding his work shirt up to his nose, which was bleeding, possibly broken. Out from the driveway, Crazy Harry was following him, yelling, 'That guy was trying to steal parts off of my truck.' So you might think what he said to you was crazy, but in comparison to the recent past, that ain't shit! The part that's worrisome is that his periods of calm are usually interrupted with periods of fucking looney tunes, and it looks and sounds like it's looney tunes time again!"

Lee and Cliff turned and looked at each other several times during Freddie's narrative and saying nothing. They both knew he would not make up such a story. Besides the shit he was saying was so fucking bizarre that it had to be true.

"I believe everything you just said to us," Cliff began, "but you should have seen the look in his eyes. It's like they went from fucking crazy to a moment of clarity once he began to speak. And knowing what we have been through the last couple of days, it kinda trips me out."

"Me too," Lee added.

"You guys are just freaking each other out over nothing. The guy is straight nuts! Trust me. He is crazier than cat shit!"

"Anyways, let's go the back way to your house. I owe Dean some money, and I want to stop by the shop before it closes," said Freddie.

"No problem," answered Cliff. Up went the volume on the radio, and appropriately, "Crazy Train" by Ozzy Osbourne was playing.

CHAPTER 23

Pablo Escobar had earned his way to being one of the biggest drug lords of his time, if ever, not by kissing asses and shaking hands. He had earned it at gun point and through brutal force. Pablo was responsible for hundreds of deaths on his way to the top, and there would be hundreds more if that's what it took to stay there, and certainly hundreds more if someone grew the balls big enough to try and overtake his position of power and wealth. Everyone who worked for him knew that for certain, so no one was willing to make that move.

He had sat at his desk longer than usual before pulling the plug, giving the orders to have someone who had crossed him killed, partly for doing him wrong and partly as a reminder of what could happen if you fucked with him and or his money. This time was different though. He had entered into an agreement. Although there were no signed documents to prove it, with a man, if he so choose, could be very dangerous himself and certainly had all the money and men it would take to retaliate should he felt it prudent.

With his feet up on his desk and leaning back in his chair, he had sat motionless, staring out the window at his herd of black rhinos, his private collection, the only such herd outside the continent of Africa and then back again at the satellite phone sitting within arm's reach, for what seemed like an eternity to him. He was contemplating whether he should make that call now or exercise some patience, waiting for his new friend to call him first and inform him that the mistake had been made, and a quickly as it had been made, it had been corrected, and that his thirty million dollars was now resting in a new location so that he could put into motion whatever it was that would allow him to pick up what was agreed upon, which was what was owed him; what was his!

Pablo didn't get to the top because he was stupid, and thus, he would wait, not very much longer, but he would wait for his new friend to make it right, to fix this mess. Then he would call, and then he would have his money. But when waiting time came down to action time, he would spare nothing to retrieve what was his. No one treated Pablo like a punk, and if they did, they would never live to talk about it.

CHAPTER 24

The red racer eased out of town and then picked up speed as the city road turned to country. Soon they would cross over the freeway (Sunset Highway, Highway 26), the true boundary line that separated the city and country's farmland. Jackson school road turned into Jackson Quarry Road on the north side of Highway 26. It would wind through farmland and pass in front of McCall's Tire and Wheel just before it intersected with Helvetia Road. They referred to it as the backway only because it was the long way to Helvetia Road, but really, it was just another, depending on where you started from.

At McCall's Tire and Wheel you could get anything in the way of tires and wheels for your car, yet its specialty was in tractor and big rig tires and wheels for farmer's trucks. The shop was located out in the sticks; some would refer to it as North Plains and others would call it Helvetia. The truth of it all is that the shop, which sat right next to the house the McCall's lived in, was really a place all its own.

The shop was a big corrugated metal building, sort of a mint green in color, which matched the residence. It was owned by Bill McCall. His staff included his son Dean; long-time employee Big Joe, for all the obvious reasons; and a guy named Arty (Dean referred to him as Flash). No one besides Bill, really knew if he was on the payroll or if he was just part of the scenery. Arty was always doing something, and always, it was hard to tell what or to what end.

Dean worked his ass off at the shop when he wasn't in school or playing football. At 6'3", he was also a fixture on the high school basketball team. He always had a chew in his lip and a joke on his mind. Because he worked for his dad and made pretty good money, he had all the toys that boys liked. The car he drove to school, a 1965 Buick Skylark Super Sport, was a nice little hot rod. His 1970 Dodge

Challenger was another story. Built from the ground up, it was most likely the fastest car in the county. It had a 440 Hemi engine in it that came out of a Dodge Charger. Using the word "fast" to describe that car was not doing it justice. The McCalls loved their automobiles, and the faster the better.

The red racer pulled up in front of the tire shop as the doors were being pulled down and locked. Dean was out front, talking to his dad, and making the last customer of the day laugh as he headed toward his car. Bringing your car into that shop to get new tires for your car will get you, on top of that, free of charge, a lot of laughs and a few more jokes to take home with.

"What's up, Deano?" Freddie said to him as he turned and started walking toward Cliff's car.

"Hard dicks and helicopters," Dean replied with a big, toothy smile. "Sorry we are closed for the evening."

"So then should I just hold that fifty bucks I owe you until tomorrow?"

"No, I will take it tonight. We are always open to receive money."

"Got change for a hundred?"

"Come into the shop, and we can find out. Besides, it's been awhile since you guys have seen the Challenger. She's all done. Well, all done except for Nitrous System. I have it. I just haven't installed it yet."

"Do you really think its needs Nitrous?" asked Cliff.

"You never know. Could happen."

"So how much do you think you have wrapped up in that hot rod?" asked Cliff.

"Not really sure. A lot of it is time."

"Would you ever sell it?"

"Maybe for the right price."

"What would that price be?" Cliff continued, and Lee and Freddie could see the wheels start to turn inside Cliff's head. They could sense where this conversation was leading.

"I would say around the ten thousand dollar mark. That's without the Nitrous. Twelve with the Nitrous and that's fully installed." All at once, they all started doing the math in their heads. Four thousand each to go in thirds. Cliff looked at them; they looked at him. All three gave the nod to each other.

Cliff asked, "Do you take cash?"

"That would be preferred method of payment," Dean replied.

Freddie jumped in. "So it's for sale then?"

"Are you three unemployed clowns saying you want to buy this car and that you want to pay cash?"

"Maybe. Would you do it?"

"I'll tell you what. If you can pay cash, I'll do the whole thing. Nitrous installed for an even ten grand. Cash on the barrelhead."

"Can you have it ready by tomorrow morning?"

"Are you three just playing games with me?"

"What do you think, guys?" Cliff asked Lee and Freddie.

"We are still waiting to hear if it can be ready by tomorrow morning." They both looked at Dean.

"Throw in five hundred more, and it will be done by morning."

"Sounds like we have a deal then."

All three started pulling wads of money out of their pockets, and one by one, each of them peeled four grand off of their money rolls that were mostly made of crispy one hundred dollar bills.

"Jesus Christ!" Dean said. "You guys rob a bank or hit the lottery?"

"Here you go. It's the original twelve grand you said you would take, but you have to throw in the extra set of tires and wheels. I know you have for this beast."

"What the fuck? Are these things real? Is this a joke?"

"It's real. The bills are real, and this is not a joke. We will be by in the morning to pick it up. Is 10:00 a.m. good for you?"

"Hell yeah! See you at ten!"

As Dean stood there wide eyed and with twelve grand cash in his hand, they jumped into the red racer and headed up the hill.

"What did your friends want?" Bill asked.

You wouldn't believe me if I told you. Has Big Joe left yet? I need him to help me with my Nitrous System."

"Nope. If you hurry, you can catch him."

Dean ran.

CHAPTER 25

Agents Smith and Smith had been waiting in their hotel room for over twenty-four hours when the call came in late night.

They sat across from each other at the hotel room's table, drinking beer that one of them had run down to the local 7-11 and picked up a few hours ago. When he had returned the poker game had continued. Smith Number 1 was up on Smith Number 2 by over a hundred dollars. Number 2 would not allow the game to end, stating that Number 1 had to give him a chance to win it back. That was over another hundred dollars ago, and unless Number 2 caught Number 1 dealing from the bottom off the deck, the bloodletting was only going to get worse.. Number 2 should have figured this out when Number 1 had been more than happy to continue with their session, putting up no resistance or trying to collect the ever growing debt, for this is the way their card games always went. Number 2 would not lose by lack of trying, but he would never win.

Along with what was being called a poker table, each room was decorated the same. A single queen-sized bed though they had requested kings, a 27-inch color tube TV, fridge, and microwave oven. Above each of their beds hung the exact piece of artwork. They had often wondered is this what the artist was aiming for. The same piece of work in every single hotel room. Both of them had complained to the front desk that there was no courtesy bar in the room, and both were annoyed even more when informed that those only came in the room that had king-sized beds. The hot tub and saunas were all being serviced, and the pool was currently empty though they were informed it would be filled and ready for use soon. Nothing about this hotel seemed to be in working order, and twelve hours into their stay, the air-conditioner in Number 2's rooms had stopped pumping cold air, and currently, the air coming out wasn't even cool, so most of the time he was in Number 1's room, playing cards and not wanting to stop, more because he had no air conditioning than about winning his money back. Number 1 didn't know this fact, but he was definitely wanting some alone time to rest and order one of those porn movies that was being advertised on the hotel's many channels.

When the call came in, it startled them both and reminded them of why they were really in that hellhole to begin with.

"Hello," Smith Number 1 answered the phone. It was his phone after all, and he did have a slight level of seniority over Number 2, a fact that he never let Number 2 forget.

"Yes, sir," he responded into the handset that was pressed up against his ear.

Then there came an "okay" a couple of more "yes, sirs" then followed by an "I think so" and an "absolutely, sir." When it came time to say good-bye, he only stood there holding the handset out in front of him and blankly staring at it. Obviously, the person at the other end had hung up on him upon issuing the orders. Next there came a long pause, the handset was placed back into its cradle and Number 2 was acting like a puppy dog humping his leg for information about what was said.

"Here is our orders," Number 1 started. "We have been instructed to first go buy new clothes that suggest we are Californians up here, looking to sink the money we made from the sale of our houses into Oregon farmland since prices are lower here. We can get more for our money. Once we have our clothes, we are to go to the local Hertz auto rental store and pick up our car that is already reserved for us. I was told it is a special rental provided by "a friend of the business," something more California like so that it doesn't look like a rental. After that, we go on a fact-finding mission. Our only clue is a place named the Stumble Inn. We go hang out at the tavern to see if anybody is throwing around hundred dollar bills. Maybe ask a few questions, but not so many as to draw attention to ourselves. If we find out anything of importance. we are to report it to out superiors and then stand by for more orders. We are not to act upon our own accord because the situation is growing more critical by the hour. The national security is at risk."

Number 2 sat staring at Number 1. It was already getting late, so a trip to get clothes would have to be put off until morning. Number 2 began to deal out the next hand of cards. Number 1 thought, How in the hell am I gonna get rid of this guy? Then threw in his ante.

CHAPTER 27

When the satellite phone rang, it was sitting in Pablo's back pocket. It would not leave his side until he talked to the man at the other end. Ever since their agreement had taken place, this was the only form of communication that ever took place between them.

"Hola, amigo," Pablo answered his phone.

"Hello, friend," was the response given.

"I have been looking forward to your call. It seems as though a package of mine has come up missing."

"Yes, I have just been made aware of this, and I assure you that we are on top of it and will have your package available within the next twenty-four hours, and I am sorry to inconvenience you."

"De nada," Pablo replied. "As long as you tell me it's been taken care of, I will consider the problem fixed. Are you sure you don't need any help? I have men in place right now that could help you."

"No! No! All is fine. We will have it wrapped up very soon!" the man at the other end snapped back. The last thing he needed was some of Pablo men killing people across the northwestern corner of the United States. He said to himself as he fiddled with his jelly beans and picking out his favorite flavors.

"Okay, then just let me know when and where to pick it up, and then we shall continue with business as usual.

"You will be the first to know."

"That works for me."

Both men hung up their phones, not bothering to say good-bye. Although they greeted one another as friend, they were far from it and always would be. One man was a notorious drug kingpin and the other one was the president of the United States of America, leader of the free world.

As the President tossed back a couple more jelly beans, he wondered how long he could hold Pablo back from shooting people all over the state of Oregon. Also how in the hell did he end up in bed with a monster like Pablo and how was he going to make it out and still keep it under wraps? There was going to be an election next year, one that he intended on winning. He liked it here in the White House. There were still so many things left to do, and he was gonna be damned if some third-world drug lord tried to get in his way.

The President sat alone in his office, looking out the window and into the rose garden, daydreaming and thinking to himself, *Why in the hell do they make licorice-flavored jelly beans? If I wanted licorice, I would have licorice on my desk and not jelly beans,* he thought as he threw a handful of black jelly beans into the trash can.

CHAPTER 28

As the full moon began to rise and the dark of night took its place in the sky Cliff, Lee, and Freddie ate a bowl of Lisa's famous chicken noodle soup while sucking down a couple of cold beers.

Cliff's mom, Lisa, was about as cool as a mother of a teenage boy could be. One reason was her letting him have the guest house all to himself for his senior year of high school, and second was that she would buy them beer. They had to pay for it out of their own pockets, or sometimes, she would allow them to work it off up at the farm, feeding cows, mowing the lawn, or shoveling cow shit. As of late, just paying cash was working just fine. All she asked of them was that after drinking, they didn't leave the property. As long as they stayed up on the farm, she figured they couldn't get into much or any trouble, and for the most part, they abided by that rule. That night, however, was going to be one of those nights when they would bend it slightly. Actually, they were going to completely shatter it.

"So check this baby out!" announced Cliff as he held up the biggest pipe bomb any of them had made or even seen.

"Jesus H. Christ!" exclaimed Freddie. Lee said nothing, only shook his head.

"I think this outta be big enough to take it down," said Cliff with a laugh, holding it up like he was hoisting an NBA championship trophy.

He called it a baby, but it looked more like a monster! A six inch long piece of galvanized plumbing pipe full of triple f black powder. It had both ends capped off and a three feet length of cannon fuse dangling from the center of it. Six inches long and three inches in diameter, it dwarfed all other pipe bombs before it.

"This should take Berg's mailbox clean off the stand," Cliff said. "I drove down Phillips Road a few days ago and happened to notice that the new one is up and all freshly painted. Tonight's the full moon, and I say we should go blow that fucker up."

"His mailbox or his house?" Lee questioned him.

"Just the mailbox," Cliff responded although they all knew Lee was joking.

"The fuse is plenty long. Pull up your big girl panties for Christ's sake. You sound like a little girl."

"Fuck you, Cliff! That thing is outta control!"

"It's him who had laid out the challenge. Don't tell me you two aren't up for it!"

The challenge Cliff was talking about had started fairly innocently one night several months ago with a CO_2 cartridge from a BB gun, some triple F black powder, and a couple of feet of cannon fuse, not to mention, a short case of Schlitz Malt Liquor and a late night motorcycle ride. All three of them piled onto Cliff's Yamaha 100, but only after pushing it down the driveway far enough so that Lisa couldn't hear it start. On that night, no one knew whose mailbox it would be, only that someone was not going to have a whole one come morning time. They settled for the one named Berg for a couple of reasons. First beings it was a road that didn't get much traffic, so the odds of an innocent person getting hurt was low, and second, because the way the road came to a rise a good distance away, they could watch their little bomb go off. What fun is it if you can't watch it go boom? They lit the fuse and watched as the Berg's mailbox was blown clean off its stand. A few days later while driving down Phillips Road, they happened to notice, because they were looking, that the Bergs had a brand-new mailbox. Not a standard mailbox like the one they had blown up, but a heavy-duty, new, and improved model sitting neatly on its stand. That of course wouldn't do, so they waited a couple of weeks, did the sneak off of the hill on the motorcycle, and once again, they shredded the Bergs mailbox. Berg was up to the challenge and replaced it with an even more stout, heavy-duty home-made mailbox made out of ⅛ thick metal. Noticing that Berg had gone bigger and better meant that they would have to follow suit.

That was how their pipe bombs had been born. Scrapping the CO2 cartridge, they stepped it up and went with some leftover plumbing pipe from repairs due to freezing pipes during a bout of below freezing weather they had experienced the previous winter.

Once again, their bomb had performed as was expected, and that was what led them to where they were tonight. They placed the new pipe bomb into a backpack, grabbed a lighter, and headed to the barn towards their waiting ride. It was close to 1:00 a.m., and it was a pretty good bet that Cliff's mom was in bed, asleep for the night. They pushed the motorcycle to the end of the driveway and coasted down the hill until they met the first rise in the road. Only there, they fired it up. On their way back, they would shut it down once they got near the house. Pushing it back up the hill on the way back was the only part of the trip they were not looking forward to. That part sucked!

Off they rode, all three, on Cliff's Yamaha 100 into the night, pushing the motorcycle to its limit, making a beeline for the Berg's mailbox. At the end of Bishop Road, they turned left and headed south on Helvetia Road. After flying by the tavern that was getting ready to close up for the night, they passed under the train trestle, hung a left, and sped down Phillips Road. Close to a mile later, they came over the rise and could see their target sitting in the distance. They always did a fly by first then they would double back, so they were headed in the right direction for the quick getaway to Bishop Road and then to their home base on top of Ritter Hill.

Cliff slowed the bike down as they rolled past their target. If they could have seen each other's faces as they went by, they all would have seen the same thing, faces that went from happy to sad. Cliff whipped a 180 and roared past it as he headed for home. Mr. Berg had taken an eight-inch cast iron pipe that was eighteen inch long and a half an inch thick, cut the ends back at a 45 degree angle and left both ends open. There was no way to blow it up short of using a C4 plastic explosives. Berg had won, and they all knew it. The only thing there was left to do was to head back to the hill and lick their wounds. The disappointment would soon be washed away with a few beers and a couple of bong hits.

CHAPTER 29

Sleep did not come easy for them that night, and when it did come, it was filled with restless dreams of money and fun. The next day would be their first big day playing with their first big purchase. They had told Dean they would be by to pick it up at 10:00 a.m. By 7:30 a.m., all three of them, after getting up with the sun, had showered, dressed, and were three beers closer to the fun side of drunk. Freddie was only two beers on his way, putting on the brakes before climbing behind the wheel of the beast they would be picking up that day. He had called dibs in driving it first, and if he had his way there would be a second.

At 10:00 a.m. on the dot, the red racer was pulling into the front parking lot of McCall's Tire and Wheel. Cliff was just about to shut the car off when Dean appeared from behind the shop and waved them around the north side of the building. Right away, you could tell that Dean and Big Joe were just dropping the hood and running a soft cloth along the front of the car. Not only had they installed the Nitrous System, but the black paint job had been buffed to a mirror shine so deep that you could have done your morning shave on it. Never before had a car shined so nicely. The old Dodge Challenger had never looked so fast!

Dean stood next to the Challenger, looking at his reflection in the paint job. He looked misty-eyed like a father sending his first born off into the big world to the college life. It was like a baby to him, but Dean was Dean, and if history proves anything about how the future will be, his next toy would be parked in the spot this one left by the end of the day.

"Here's the keys, boys. Who gets honors?" As Freddie raised his hand, Dean tossed him the keys and then said, "Get honor and stay honor" with a little chuckle "Hit the bottom button on the right, it's the auto start, so you can warm this baby up before you even get to the door. The left one is for the door locks. It's twice for the trunk too," Dean explained. "So you have to tell me, boys. Where in the hell did you get all that money?"

"Well, Deano." Freddie was the first to speak up. "We could tell you but then we would have to kill ya."

All three busted up laughing. If only that line would work on Cliff's mom.

With all of the pleasantries out of the way, Freddie hit the start button, and he fired up right away. Then the door locks, and then they all piled in. Seconds later, they were gone like smoke.

Freddie hung a right when he reached the end of the parking lot and then headed south into town. They figured they should put off going up on the hill until Cliff figured out what he was going to tell his mom. As soon as they were on black top, Freddie punched it, and smoke boiled off of the tires; but once they gripped the road, they were shot off down the road like they were released from a slingshot. The car had incredible power, and they had to peel themselves out of the back of their seats.

"Jesus H. Christ1 This thing is fast!" yelled Freddie.

"Keep it between the ditches!" Cliff yelled back. "I wanna turn!"

Like a bullet, they were on their way into town, a trip that would take half the time it usually took. All Cliff could think about was what he was going to tell his mother. First things being first though, it was time to head over to Frank's house and see how things were coming along with those Discs.

CHAPTER 30

When they arrived at Franks, he was down in the basement, but where else would he be? Walking in without so much as a knock, they entered like they always did, catching Frank with his pants down, watching porn on the Internet.

"Now we know why you never leave the basement," Lee said, laughing.

It certainly looked exactly how Lee had called it. There were dishes stacked up by the door, enough to overflow the red recycling bin, and an Albertson's grocery shopping basket. It must have been over a weeks' worth. Frank never took them up to the kitchen on the main floor of the house where his parents lived. The dishes would sit there, growing mold on top of the dried up remnants of leftover food until his mother, not his father, who was just as lazy as Frank, like father like son, would come downstairs and haul them upstairs all by herself. And that didn't happen until there were no more clean dishes anywhere in the house. Frank's mother was no less lazy than the men in her life once she had married and once she had given birth to who was also the reason she had to get married in the first place. It was a continuous three-way contest to see who could be the least productive. So far, the men were winning, but only because Momma, who weighed 350 pounds, if she wasn't holding a ten pound turkey up to her mouth gnawing on it. She claimed to eat due to her pent-up sexual frustrations. Frank's dad would say that they didn't fuck because they were all out of flour to roll her in so he could locate the wet spot. It was obvious that as long as she ate, she would not get any dick, and if she got no dick, she was going to keep eating. They were caught in a vicious cycle for sure, and that vicious cycle was what drove their son to spend his days and his nights watching Internet porn and jacking off into endless rolls of paper towels, vowing never to end up like his parents.

"Fuck you, guys," Frank replied while pulling up his pants and throwing a paper towel into the overflowing trashcan. "I was only cleaning off my monitor!"

"You have to have your pants down to clean your monitor?" asked Lee with another laugh.

"We all agree you're a funny guy. I suppose you guys are here about your fucking Discs? Did I ever ask you three if you knew how to knock?"

"You never have asked us that, but believe me, we will from now on!" Lee finished.

"So you mentioned those Discs. What's going on there?" Cliff asked. "I am guessing they weren't full of porn."

"Everyone's a comedian today."

"The discs?"

"Yeah, right, the discs. I have been having some trouble cracking the encryption code. It's like none I have ever seen before. Where did they come from that might help?"

Freddie chimed in. "We could tell you, but then we would have to kill you."

"That makes it three for three. You guys are more fun than a barrel of monkeys"

"That might be giving us a little bit more credit than we deserve. Might!"

"That probably true," Frank replied.

"So now you're the funny guy?"

"Check it out. You guys are going to have to give me more time with these discs. I am gonna check on the Internet for a program to get into them with. Now if I was told where they came from, that search would go a lot easier, but apparently, that's a secret of national security level, and therefore, you guys won't tell me. Anyway, I suppose you're wanting to make my job tougher."

"Come on, Frank. You know that's not why, and if we did tell you, you wouldn't believe us anyway," Cliff said. "If you need more time then you need more time. We are not trying to push you. We just happened to be in town, so we stopped by."

"Cool! Maybe stop by later on, or better yet, tomorrow. I should know something by then. It's also possible that I won't be able to crack them open at all."

"Well, that's enough of that kind of talk," Cliff shot back.

"I am just saying it's possible."

"I hear you, Frank. Keep trying, and when we come by, maybe we will have more information. You may have better luck if you didn't have to clean your monitor so often."

"Fuck you! All three of you! If you learned how to knock, you wouldn't see me cleaning my monitor, would you?" Frank said. "And that's not a question!"

All three of them climbed the stairway on the way out of Frank's basement, laughing as they went along their way to the car and passing Frank's mom on her way down to pick up the dishes.

"You may want to knock." Freddie said as they passed her by. "Frank might be cleaning his monitor." Freddie was now laughing.

"I'll tell you what. It seems like every time I go down there, he is cleaning his monitor," she replied. "Do monitors always get so dirty?"

All three of them were now laughing almost hysterically.

"Maybe you should ask him," Lee finally said.

CHAPTER 31

"Okay, check it out, Cliff. I know it's your turn to drive, but I really want to go by Jenny's house. We don't need to hang out or even stop there, just roll by really slow and then send up some smoke from the tires. I just want to wave to her from the car when she looks out the window. Okay?" Freddie said, almost begging.

Cliff turned at the intersection, throwing up a little smoke as he did a 180 and then headed toward Jenny's house, knowing that if he didn't, the constant begging and whining would not end until they did as he asked.

Turning down Jenny's street, Cliff crawled down the road into a slow roll and then stopped completely. If he was to put on a show, it may as well be a good one. While holding the brake pedal down all the way, Cliff started easing down on the gas, and soon he was in full power brake mode with smoke pouring off of the tires, encasing the whole car in a cloud of white smoke. When the smoke cleared, there she was—a thing of beauty and the subject of a teenage boy's fantasy—peering out the house's front window. Freddie waved to her and smiled. When Jenny smiled and waved back, Cliff put the pedal to the metal, leaving a cloud bank of smoke rolling toward her house. They just waved with grins going from ear to ear. For once, with that girl, Freddie was getting the attention he had desired for so long. They disappeared in a cloud of smoke.

CHAPTER 32

Jenny's mother looked out of her upstairs bedroom window to see what all the commotion was about, and when she did, she caught a glimpse of Freddie waving out the passenger side window of a shiny black hot rod just before a blanket of smoke enveloped the car.

Jenny's mom, Maddie, was exactly what you would think she was, blonde, beautiful, and sharp as a tack. It was easy to guess where Jenny's good looks and brains came from.

As Maddie came walking down the stairs, she was saying, "Was that Freddie in that car, showing off for you?"

"He wasn't showing off for me, Mother!"

"You're right. He was probably showing off for that cop that lives across the street. How silly of me to think differently," Maddie continued. "When is that boy gonna get tired of you shitting on him all of the time?"

"Mother, I do not shit all over Freddie!"

"Is that so?"

"Yes, Mother, that is so!"

"Then let me ask you a couple of questions. Isn't he the guy you backed out on those two movie dates last year? And isn't he the guy you leave hanging when you think you have found another new boyfriend?"

"That's not shitting on him, Mother! Freddie and I are just friends, and he knows that."

"I just don't get it, Jenny. That guy bends over backward for you, and sometimes, you won't give him the time of day."

"Mother, you make it sound like I am so mean to him."

"Well, aren't you?"

"No!"

"Really?"

"Yes!"

"So while you are out chasing other guys around, Freddie is the one who, without fail, walks you home from school every day, carries your books every day. When you're sick, he always brings you homework to you. When one of your new boyfriends gets caught cheating on you, he's the one who keeps you company, and when one of your boyfriends breaks up with you to chase some new girl, Freddie comes by to cheer you up. Most people, my dear girl, would call that a perfect boyfriend."

"Mother, are you just about done?"

"Just two more questions and then I will be done."

"Okay, but only two."

"How come Freddie never has a steady girl friend?"

"Because they always get mad at him for walking me home all the time, but I don't ask him to do it, Mother. He does it all on his own."

"If Freddie walked out of your life tomorrow, how would you feel about that? And I want an honest-to-God, truthful answer to this question, Jenny."

Jenny went silent for a few minutes, so she could think this question over, but every time she tried to answer, pools of tears welled up in her eyes, and soon they were rolling down her porcelain-colored cheeks and then falling to the ground.

"That's what I thought. Let me tell you something that comes from a girl-woman who really knows what she is talking about."

"You said only two more questions!"

"That was only two questions, now I am going to give you a piece of advice. That boy has been standing in the batter's box for years, just waiting to get into the game. Inning after inning, you keep giving all those other guys a free pass to start rounding the bases while Freddie tries to earn a swing of the bat."

"I don't let any guys go around all of the bases, Mother!" Jenny said, interrupting her mom. "I am not saying you do, and you are missing the point. Next year is your senior year, and when you get to the end of it, things are going to happen. Everybody is going to start going their separate ways. Some will go to college, some will join the service, some will find a job and start working on their careers, and some will do whatever else there is to do. And when that happens, you might not see Freddie ever again. And if you do see him, it will probably be at a class reunion, and there will most likely be another woman on his arm. Everybody likes to play in the game, and if you won't let him, you can bet your ass that he will find another team to play on that will let him out of that batter's box, so he can take a swing at the ball."

"You know that I hate sports, Mother!" Jenny said while running up to her bedroom and then slamming the door all the way. She had streams of tears running down her face.

CHAPTER 33

Morning was giving way to afternoon, and Lee's stomach was starting to growl. Each of them still had their pockets lined with one hundred dollar bills, and it seemed like now that they could afford to eat anywhere. The decision was harder to make.

"Let's go to Mickey D's. I'm buying," Lee said. "Anything you want."

"Are you fucking kidding me? You have a couple grand in your pocket, and the best you can do is Mickey D's?" Cliff replied.

"What's wrong with McDonalds?" Freddie asked as he joined into the decision-making process. "Besides, you were the one who said we should take it easy and not be throwing money around."

"I know," Lee exclaimed. "Why don't we head up to the tav and have a jumbo burger, onion rings, and a pitcher of beer?"

"I think I can afford it or you fags could join me for a game of pool to decide who picks up the check."

"Well, shit. That's pretty much locks it up as far as you buying us lunch goes." Cliff laughed and Freddie smiled in agreement.

Cliff pointed the hot rod north and left the city behind. As they cruised along, they also turned on the car stereo for the first time. Dean had installed a high-dollar tape deck with AM/FM radio, a 500 watt amplifier, and awesome speakers all made by Alpine. The car filled with sounds as they traveled along. AC/DC's "Have a Drink on Me" poured from the speakers. Cliff and Freddie looked at Lee and then started to laugh. Lee lifted up the middle finger of his right hand. It was impossible to tell if he said it out loud or if he only mouthed it. But either way, he had just told them both to fuck off!

CHAPTER 34

A cab pulled up to the store front of Boot Leg. It was a local store located close to the airport. Out of the cab climbed two men, both named Smith, and both wearing their signature Secret Service suits.

The bell at the door clanged as they entered, bringing the clerk scrambling from the back room to the front counter and offering her assistance. Carla was her name, and she quickly pointed the two strangers toward their latest selection of men's country and western clothes and accessories. Before too long, Carla was ringing up a few changes in clothes, boots, belts, and cowboy hats totaling $1,235.95, A bonanza day for the local store owner. Carla even threw in a complimentary ice cream cone with the deal. Smith Number 1 declined the offer. Smith Number 2 did not and actually accepted Number 1's cone too and strolled out of the store and to the cab while fisting the two ice cream freebies.

As they came out of the store, the cabbie was quick to notice their appearance and their new change of clothes.

"Howdy, partner" the cabbie said with a smile. "Perfect timing cause the stage coach was getting ready to leave."

"We are paying you to drive, buddy, not to be a comedian," replied Number 1.

"Not a problem, buckaroo. I'll throw in the jokes for free," he said, laughing more.

"Just drive us to the local Hertz Rent-a-Car."

"Not the nearest rodeo?"

"I suppose they have your mustangs tied up out front of the rental office?"

"Why don't you just come right out and say you don't want a tip," Number 1 said, obviously annoyed.

"Sorry, pal. I was just trying to be cordial."

"Well, you can stop anytime."

The rest of the cab ride was made in silence if not for the constant licking sounds coming from Number 2 and his ice cream cones. As they pulled into the parking lot, it was easy to see which rental car was waiting for them, and it definitely was not a Mustang.

Their car was fire-engine red and sparkling clean. The sunshine bounced off the paint job with a blinding effect. The black colored rag top was in the open position, and they could smell the aroma of Italian leather in the air. The odometer read fifteen miles. The brand-new Austin Martin was the crown jewel of that parking lot. It was the first year they made the two-door sedan although the backseat didn't resemble anything like one.

As Number 1 entered the lobby of the rental car store, the agent informed them that the keys were in it, the papers had already been signed by fax machine, and they were all ready to go. When Hertz said express rental, they meant it.

Number 2 loaded their shopping bags into the trunk and was getting ready to climb into the driver's seat when Number 1 came out of the store and ordered him to the passenger's seat.

"Oh no, Smith. I will be driving this baby. You might get a chance later, but I am first!" said Number 1.

Number 2 turned his head when Number 1 gave his orders and dripped ice cream onto the driver's seat. He was about to say something and decided to say, "Fuck it," instead and walked around to the passenger side.

"What the fuck!" cried Number 1 as he sank his ass down into the driver's seat.

"Sorry," was all Number 2 said and then a small grin appeared on his face.

Number 1 handed Number 2 the written directions to the Stumble Inn and then pointed the car out of the parking lot, punched it and ice cream fell into Number 2's lap, and "Sorry" was all Number 1 said grinning.

"Don't fuck with the bull son because you may just get the horn!"

"Fuck off!" replied Number 2 as he threw his ice cream, or what was left of it, out of the car and into the street. He then picked up the directions and started to navigate.

Hertz was on the west side of town, so they followed the Jackson School Road out of town and toward the Sunset Highway. As they traveled north across the freeway and continued down Jackson Quarry Road, their brand-new rental car bottomed out just before the tire shop as they crossed the train tracks and were making an awful noise as they pulled into the front parking area of McCall's Tire and Wheel.

Dean walked out and met the men before they even got out of the car.

"Sounds like you fellas found the railroad tracks," said Dean.

As they stepped out of the car, Number 1 replied, "Don't you think they should fix those things?"

"Been thinking that for years," said Dean. "And what brings you cowboys out this far north? The California boarder is about five hundred miles south of here."

"Not who, what!" replied Dean.

"Either that or my dad forgot to tell me it was Western days at work today, or maybe the rodeo is in town. Take your pick."

"So I take it everyone in the area is a comedian?"

"You dress like that, pilgrim, and somebody gonna say something."

"Could you save the comments and see what is wrong with our car, please?"

"Sure enough. I'll lift 'er up, but I can tell you what's wrong with her already."

"Yeah, what's that?" said Number 2.

"Same thing always happens every time some city slicker comes barreling over them train tracks and then pulls in here. Sounds like you threw out your high-speed muffler bearings," Dean replied while walking around to the back of the car, pulling out a little bottle of oil from his back pocket and then dripping some onto the ground. "Looks like you are dripping some turn signal fluid on the ground. You two must a been hauling ass over them tracks."

95

"Can you fix it?"

"Sure can if you got an hour or so to spare."

"Yeah, can't really drive it like that," said Number 1.

"Hey, Big Joe, you wanna give me a hand out front?" Dean yelled into the shop.

"Sure thing, Deano. I'll be right there," Big Joe replied.

They called the guy Big Joe for a reason. Dean himself was 6'3" and weighed around 230 pounds, and when Big Joe stood next to him, he made Dean look like a midget. If he didn't duck as he passed through the doorway, he would hit his head and the doorway as he was 6'6" high. "Whatcha got here, Deano?" asked Big Joe.

"These city slickers can't read the signs that have railroad crossing written all over 'em and threw out their high-speed muffler bearings and are also leaking some turn signal fluid."

"Another one of those, huh?" said Big Joe as he brought around the floor jack and also the air wrench and a big grin painted across his bearded face.

"If you can get her jacked up, I am gonna go get that bearing out from the office."

"So what part of California are you fellas from?" asked Big Joe.

"Who says we're from California?" Number 1 responded.

Big Joe only glanced at them and started jacking up the rear of the car. Once he was done, Big Joe said, "I did, didn't you hear me?"

"Maybe we should just go wait inside the office while you two work on the car," Number 1 replied as they both slowly backed away from the big man.

"That might be the best idea you two have had all day," Big Joe shot back.

Bill McCall met them when they entered into the front office area. He only glanced at them, went back to his paperwork, and without looking up, asked them if they had been helped yet already knowing the answer.

"Yes," was the only response from Number 1.

"Hey mister your soda machine just ate my dollar bill," said Number 2.

Without looking up, Bill said "It says right there the machine's out of order. Seems to me you cowpokes outta be paying a lot closer attention to whatcha all are doing."

Number 1 gave Number 2 a look that could only mean, "I can't wait to get the fuck out of this place."

As Dean lay under their car, pulling the trigger of the air wrench from time to time while Big Joe walked back and forth from the shop, bringing back a different tool each time, pretending like they were hard at work.

"So how much you gonna charge these two genius'?" Big Joe asked Dean.

"Not sure yet. This is about a hundred thousand dollar car, so I am thinking about hitting pretty hard. What do you think?" The discussion continued while they acted like they were working for close to thirty minutes. Finally, Dean climbed out from under the car. Big Joe lowered it to the ground, and then they both walked into the office.

Dean pounded on the keys of the resister and then announced. "That'll be $1,500.00 cash!"

"Are you fucking kidding me!" yelled Number 1.

"You could always take it up with our complaint department. He's standing right behind you."

As Big Joe moved closer and closer, they dug into their pockets and pulled out all their cash.

"All we got is $1,215 cash between us."

"I guess that'll have to do," said Dean.

"You can just owe us the rest."

All five men walked out to the front of the shop, and Number 1 and Number 2 started to climb into their little sports car and was saying their good-byes when, from around the bend of the road came the Challenger. They could hear it before they could see it. They came to a stop, still sitting in the middle of the road.

"What's up, Deano?" Cliff yelled. "City slicker, throw out another high-speed muffler bearing? Or was it the turn signal fluid this time?"

"Both!" Dean yelled back and watched as Cliff gunned it and took off like a bullet.

"That's a pretty nice hot rod," Number 2 exclaimed.

"Sure is," Dean said. "I just sold it to them yesterday. Paid cash, my favorite."

"All cash? That must have been over ten thousand dollars, judging by your prices."

Dean laughed. "Pretty close. They paid twelve Gs."

Number 1 looked over at Number 2 and the wheels started turning in their heads.

"Ya, think it's faster than this car?" they asked.

"Maybe close on the drag strip, but yours be faster if there was any corners but—"

Number 1 cut him off. "So you think we could take it in a race?"

"Maybe but—"

They cut him off again. "You think they would race us? Say for pink slips?"

"Maybe you would have to ask them, but you may want to consider…"

They cut him off a third time, and Dean was getting pissed!

"Where might we find them?"

"Try the Stumble Inn. They are usually there."

"That's where we are headed for lunch. We hear they have the best burgers around."

"Then you hear right," Dean responded as all three men turned and headed toward the office to split their money three ways and drink a beer.

"So, Dean, you think they should let you tell them about the Nitrous we put in that thing?" Big Joe asked.

"I tried. City folks always too busy to listen. Here's your four hundred, and here's yours, Dad."

As Dean handed them their money, they all laughed. Big Joe handed out cold beers that they stored in the soda machine.

"You know, you woulda got 'em for $1,216 if they wouldn't have put a dollar in the soda machine," said Bill.

"Did you tell 'em it don't take money? You can just pull 'em out for free?" asked Dean.

"Nope. They never asked!" Bill said and they busted out laughing.

CHAPTER 35

South of the border, Pablo Escobar waited patiently inside his jungle hideaway mansion for a call from his new friends in the United States to provide him with new coordinates so that he could send his men to get his cash and then return to the jungle with his money.

At the very same time, several thousand miles away, the President waited for the very same news so he could pass it along, hopefully, to keep Pablo from sending in his men to fix the problem and leave a trail of dead bodies in their wake of destruction.

On the other side of the US, Pablo's men were at the ready, awaiting orders. The guns were cleaned and loaded. If that call came now, they could be on their way in mere minutes. As they waited, they watched CNN. It seems that more bodies were found along the side of some jungle road in South America, and they were linking them to the Columbian cartel. They suddenly became homesick.

The phone ringing startled them back into reality. On other end of the phone Pablo issued his orders. "I want you two to make a little visit to the Stumble Inn. Have a beer and something to eat. These Americans are taking too long in getting my money back. See if you can pick up some information so we can handle this ourselves. Play it low-key. Do not draw attention to yourselves!"

CHAPTER 36

The black Challenger sat in the parking lot all by itself toward the back, not wanting any other car doors to ding its paint job. Even standing still, it looked fast.

Smith Number 1 pulled the brand-new Austin Martin into the space next to the Challenger; actually, there were no painted spaces for the lot was made of gravel, so as the little red car parked next to the black one, it seemed to be trespassing on its personal space.

They entered the tav, one behind the other, and moseyed on toward the back where three kids seemed to be arguing over a game of billiards.

Number 1 spoke to them first. "That your hot rod out there?"

All three turned their heads and then turned back to their game without a response.

"I asked you if that was your hot rod out there, son!"

All three again looked at them and, without a response, went back to their game.

"Lookie there, guys, it's the two dumbasses from the tire shop," Cliff said to his friends, ignoring the two strangers. "Hey, Freddie, how much you think Dean got these two cowboys for this time?"

Freddie laughed. "If history is any way to tell the future, I would have to say $1,000 unless, that is, he also topped off their turn signal fluid then he got 'em for $1,500 cash!"

To that, all three of them gave out a laugh.

"Look here, you little smartass," said Number 1 and started walking toward Cliff and Freddie. Before he could reach them, Lee stepped in between them with his cue raised. "I think you boys outta go take a seat and cool down before things get to serious around here."

The two Smiths noticed two other big boys toward the front of the Tavern getting restless but didn't know they were two of Lee's older brothers, both of whom were bigger than Lee.

Both men turned on their heels, stepped up to the bar, and ordered a burger, beer, and onion rings.

The three boys continued with their game of cutthroat, still not paying attention to the two men but instead talking about them in from of them. Lee hoped for a fight. Cliff and Freddie worked at it for him.

"Well, maybe they ain't so dumb after all," Cliff started in again. "You suppose that's their little red car out there or are there two horses tied up out front?"

They all laughed.

Freddie reached into his pocket and pulled out a fresh on hundred dollar bill and tossed it on the bar. "Here, this will pay for your burgers. We all know Dean cleaned out your pockets."

They all laughed again.

"So what brings you fellas up from California?" Freddie asked.

"Why does everyone keep asking us that?" Number 2 responded.

"Check it out. Every time someone comes up here to buy cheap property, the first thing they do is dress like they came from Texas. The second thing they do is hit that railroad crossing below McCall's shop, and then they're gouged by Dean for some bogus repair. Next they end up here, broke and pissed off and hungry. Usually, Randy the owner treats them on the house, but today, Randy ain't here, and his wife don't take checks or credit cards," Freddie said.

"So how did I do?" Lee asked.

"Pretty good. I suppose." Then both Smiths looked at on another. "Is that your Challenger out there?"

"Technically, it belongs to all three of us."

Instantly, Smiths memory flashed back to the photos they had of three lawn chairs sitting at the little campsite by the river.

"Looks pretty fast," said Number 1.

The two agents devised a plan on their way to the tavern where they would befriend them, race them, and then find out where they lived, thinking that's where the money and the Discs would be stashed.

"Fastest car in county!"

"Was the fastest, you mean."

"No, I don't think I stuttered or misspoke, mister. There ain't a car around here could beat it down a drag strip."

"So then, you boys wouldn't be opposed to a little race and a little wager?"

"What kind of wager, mister? We already know you emptied your pockets back at McCall's."

"How about car for car?"

"Hey, Lee!" yelled Freddie. "You think they bumped their heads coming over the tracks or they just got shit for brains?"

"Well, when we saw their car at McCall's, the top was down. So make your own conclusions." Lee answered.

"You all sure are a bunch of cocky little bastards, ain'tcha?"

"Nope! Cocky would be driving around in a sports car worth ninety grand all dressed up like Howdy Doody," Cliff shot back and then laughed. "Why don't you two rodeo clowns take your show on the road before you find yourselves walking back to Cali in them brand-new boots?"

"That's all right. I was scared once before too," shot back Number 1.

"Mister, you just lost yourselves a fancy little sports car!" Lee said before his two friends could stop him. "You tell us when and where."

"How about right now, and we race back to McCall's shop? We gotta bone to pick with him anyways."

"You're on!" shouted Lee.

"Lee!" Cliff said. "Our car is built for a drag strip not a road course."

"If you boys wanna back out, we understand."

"Fuck you, mister! Somebody call over to McCall's and tell them to hold up traffic and set up a finish line. The races are coming to town."

The call was made, the traffic was stopped, and the finish line was set.

"Go ahead and bag up their burgers, walkin' can make a man hungry," Lee told the barkeep.

Both cars sat side by side on Helvetia Road pointing north. Ahead of them lay a mile and a half of road course that would wind down to a country road, go over the hill, through more S curves, and finish where only that morning, the boys had picked up their hot rod and now sat poised to lose it. Easy come, easy go, thought Freddie.

"You can beat 'em," Lee said to Cliff.

Cliff thought to himself and then said it out loud, "Might not have to explain anything to my mom tonight."

The barkeep raised a bar towel in her hand as she stood between the two cars Beauty and the Beast.

The flag dropped, the Beast spun out, and the sports car shot forward, grabbed gears, and headed for the first set of S curves. The Challenger's tires finally grabbed the road and kept its nose about midway down the side of its opponent. Smith Number 1 shifted again and pulled out to a one-car length advantage, enough to cut of Cliff and take the lead going into the curves.

"Come on, Cliff," said Lee. "If we don't take 'em going up the hill by the church, we can kiss this car good-bye."

"Sit back and shut up, Lee. You are the one who got us here in the first place. Just watch and learn. Oh, and put on your seatbelt," Cliff shot back.

Cliff stayed on their ass when they came around the corner and started going up the hill. Every time he went for a pass, Number 1 blocked his way.

"Okay, Freddie. It looks like we better get the Nitrous ready."

"Are you thinking what I think you are thinking?"

"It's the only way."

"Pull your seatbelt tight, Lee!" Freddie yelled as he opened up the bottle and stood ready by the button.

Both cars roared, one behind the other, as they went over the top of the hill, almost close enough to touch bumpers. They were over the hill and into the last set of S curves, just before the small rise and drop that made up the intersection of Logie Trail.

"The road is too winding, Cliff. There is no way to pass 'em!" Freddie answered.

"Oh no! You guys are fucking crazy!" Lee yelled then sat back into his seat and pulled his buckle tight.

"When we get halfway up the rise, hit the button and hold it down!"

Both cars came out of the S curves like they were connected at the bumpers.

"Remember, halfway or we will ram into them," Cliff yelled.

Right as the red car crested the top of the hill Freddie hit the Nitrous button and held it down. Instantly, the car jumped forward as they came off of the ground. You could almost hear Waylon Jennings singing, "Just Good Ol' Boys" theme song from the *Dukes of Hazzard*. And when the Smiths looked in their mirrors, they saw nothing. When they looked up, all they could see was the exhaust system Dean had put on the old Dodge Challenger.

From the parking lot of McCall's shop, Big Joe says to Dean. "I think they should have listened to you trying to tell them about the Nitrous!" Dean and Big Joe laughed.

"Now if they can only slow 'er down." Dean responded.

Smith Number 1 panicked and hit the brakes when Smith Number 2 screamed. It was just enough to give the Challenger what it needed to land in front of the Austin Martin and not on top of it. The car hit the road and bounced once before Cliff slammed on the brakes. Smoke piled off his tires, blinding the Smiths, who in turn stepped on the brakes. Cliff pulled the steering wheel hard to the left and the whole car slid sideways before he stomped on the gas pedal, barely making the turn and went speeding down the last straight away towards McCall's.

A block to the left, one block to the right, and the Challenger crossed the finish line one car length in front of the red sports car.

Both cars used the turnaround driveway in front of the McCall's house then pulled in side by side in front of the tire shop.

Cliff and Freddie were the first ones to get out of the car, and Lee was right behind them.

"Did you see that shit, Dean?" Lee asked.

"Did you see us fly over those guys to win the race? Tell me you did, Dean! Tell me you did, Joe! Wasn't that the shit?"

Lee ran up and hugged both his friends, huge bear hugs that could almost knock the wind from a man's body. Lee looked like a little kid on Christmas morning.

Cliff was looking at Freddie, who walked over to the Austin Martin, pulled open the driver's side door, and yelled "First dibs on driving!"

Cliff yelled, "Shotgun!"

Lee jumped over the back of the sports car and landed in the backseat. "I don't give a fuck if I have to ride back here every fuckin time we drive this car!" Lee shouted and laughed. "Look at this fuckin' car, Dean, and it's all ours. We won it fair and square! Did you see it, Dean? Holy shit!"

Freddie invited Number 1 to "Get the fuck out of my car!"

Suddenly, Smith Number 1 started to refuse to get out, saying, "It wasn't a fair way to win!" He made a move for his service pistol hanging in his side holster.

Before he could touch it, Dean, Big Joe, and his dad pulled sawed-off shotguns from who knows where, and everything grew quiet, even Lee.

As Dean pressed his sawed-off shotgun into the cheek of Smith Number 1, he said, "Pull that hand back slowly or lose half of your face." Smith did as he was told. "Now pull out your little pistols, both of you and hand 'em over." Both did as they were told. "Now if I am hearing right, you two cowboys made the bet, lost the race, and now wanna renege on the bet?" Dean questioned them, expecting no answers and getting what is expected. "You two fellas can now step out of the car 'cause it don't belong to you anymore, and I am pretty sure you just lost any argument you was going to present." He then tucked their pistols into the back of his pants.

Both Smith's stepped out of the vehicle slowly. Freddie jumped into the driver's seat and closed the door. Cliff soon followed.

From out of the house came Dean's mom. "Oh my!" she said. "Do be careful with those guns. Dean, you know I don't like them."

"Don't worry, Lori," Dean's dad spoke up. "You know we don't put bullets in these guns. We know how much you hate 'em."

With that said, Cliff tossed Dean the keys to the Challenger, "Could you put those new tires and wheels on the car? I think we mighta have flat spotted 'em on the last corner. Oh yeah, here's their burgers, and here's some money. You may want to call them cowboys a cab."

They all laughed as Dean caught the fresh, crispy one hundred dollar bill and watched the Austin Martin along with its new owners disappear around the bend in the road.

CHAPTER 37

They sat in the back of the tavern, cloaked by the shadows of the afternoon sun. Two men were drinking beer, eating burgers, and taking in the spectacle of the two men dressed like they had stepped out of a country and western music video. Sometime eating, sometimes watching, sometimes drinking and laughing, they watched as the three youngster's poked fun at the strangers who stood out amongst the regulars in this country tavern filled with regulars and a few new customers who were hot on the trail of the best burgers in town.

All of the commotion was all that they needed to keep all of eyes off them, two Columbians at the back of the bar. They took in the laughter, the posturing, the laying down of the wager, and the finishing race, not to mention the throwing around of fresh, new one hundred dollar bills.

The matchbook one of them held in their hand had indeed led them to the right spot at the right time, placing them hot on the trail of their boss's money.

As the race began, they were able to slip out of the tavern the same way they had arrived, unnoticed. They climbed into their metallic light blue Toyota 4Runner and followed the path chosen by the racers. One drove while the other one called their boss to report their progress. They drove on in silence.

CHAPTER 38

As Freddie drove their race winnings toward town, Lee sat in the backseat, practically lying sideways for there was not enough room for the big man, and next to Freddie sat Cliff, who was silently thinking, What in the hell am I going to tell my mom now?

Cliff snapped out of his daze, leaned forward, and opened the glove box. Inside he found the rental agreement and insurance card with the name Hertz written across the top of both documents. As he read them, Freddie caught a glimpse at them as well.

"What the fuck?" Cliff said.

"I agree. What the fuck?" Freddie asked "What do you suppose that means?"

"First I would have to say they were gambling with a car that wasn't theirs. Second, I would say we are driving one that won't be ours much longer."

"That's fucked up! This car is the shit!"

"Enjoy it while you can because somebody is going to want it back sometime soon."

In silence, they drove on, then Freddie turned on the radio and tuned in KGON. "One Bourbon, One Scotch and One Beer" by George Thorogood was playing loudly through the top-of-the-line stereo system. Freddie and Cliff looked at each other when the line, "Everybody funny, now you funny too." Was sang through the multiple speakers located everywhere in the car.

Lee sang along, oblivious to the most recent findings in the glove box.

Freddie executed a couple of high-speed turns in the European sports car, aiming straight for Hillsboro.

"You are fuckin kidding me, right?" Cliff said.

No response from Freddie.

"Don't you think it's going to raise a lot of questions if she sees us in yet another car today?"

"Relax, you said yourself we wouldn't have it much longer. I will just tell her it's your dad's."

Cliff leaned forward and cranked up the radio even louder. It sounded like as good a story as any and wondered if his mom would buy that story? Looking in their mirrors, both could see Lee smiling from ear to ear, his hair blowing in the wind. They would wait till later to tell him the latest news.

Realizing that the car is only temporary, Freddie started running the shit out of it, traveling the last couple miles of back road at close to one hundred miles per hour while Cliff and Lee held on tight.

"Sorry, just wanted to see how well it handled," Freddie said, smiling. "You guys will get your turn too!"

Freddie brought the car back down to the speed limit as they entered town and then turned down Jenny's street and pulled up into her driveway. Jenny came out as they were getting out of the car and met Freddie with a hug and questions about the car, asking if Cliff's dad had gotten a new one. Neither of them answered. They were okay letting her believe what she wanted to believe, especially if they didn't have to lie to her about it.

Cliff asked, "Do I get one of those hugs too?" and then laughed as his friend shot him a sideways look.

Freddie reached into the car and grabbed the keys, moved around to the rear of the car, then slipped the key into the trunk lock and gave it a turn. Inside the trunk were several bags with the Boot Leg name and logo printed on them. Cliff began to rifle through them as everybody watched.

"What's all this stuff?" asked Lee.

"Well, buddy, we weren't going to break the news to you yet, but this is a Hertz Rental car. It wasn't those guys' car to lose or ours to win. This whole thing is temporary," said Cliff.

"What are you guys talking about? I thought you said this was Cliff's dad's car?" Jenny asked.

"Actually, you said it. We only went along with it. Sorry," Freddie explained. "Your finding this stuff out at the same time we are."

Along with the cowboy clothes they found in the trunk, there were identical-looking suits. Obviously, these were the clothes they had dressed out of before going all country and western for a disguise.

Jenny spoke up, "This is really weird, guys, because my mother's boyfriend stopped by after work the other night, telling her about this Lear jet that landed at the airport. He said that two men dressed up like they were FBI or CIA stepped off the jet and climbed into a military Hummer and left by way of the back gate. He said the whole thing looked odd to him. Now you're telling me that two strange men wearing Western clothes were messing with you at the tavern, raced you, and you find clothes matching the description of those men from the airport?" Jenny continued. "Doesn't that sound weird to you, guys? What have you gotten yourselves into?" she asked.

"What do you mean?" Freddie responded. "We haven't gotten ourselves into nothing. We were minding our own business when they started messing with us!"

"Doesn't the whole thing sound weird to you, guys?"

Cliff volleyed this one. "Sure, it sounds weird when you put it like that, but it's got to be coincidence. What would the FBI want with us three?"

"You tell me!" Jenny shot back. "It's not like you three aren't always up to something. Freddie told me about your mailbox shenanigans and…"

Freddie cut her off. "I told you that was our secret. Besides, how would the FBI know where to look for whomever blew up the mailbox?"

Freddie was now looking at Cliff and Lee with that deer-caught-in-the-headlight look.

"What the fuck, Freddie!" Cliff yelled. "What else has he told you?"

"Nothing! He told me that a couple of months ago. He hasn't told me anything since then."

Cliff gave Freddie a sideways glance of relief, but Freddie knew he was not pleased. Lee gave Freddie a friendly punch to the shoulder. A friendly punch to most people, but coming from Lee, it shot pain clear down to his hand. "Cliff said you would give us up to a female."

"It's just Jenny for Christ's sake, and I haven't told her anything else. Chill out!" Freddie said, rubbing his arm.

"Anything else like what?" Jenny asked.

"Nothing!" Cliff and Lee said at the same time.

"I think it's time for us to get going," Cliff said, and Lee agreed.

Grabbing the keys out of the trunk lock Cliff made it clear he would be driving this time.

"Be careful, you guys," Jenny said as they pulled away.

Cliff hit the gas to let Freddie know he was not pleased, and Lee had already done the same. As they disappeared around the corner, a Toyota 4Runner started up and drove past Jenny, who was standing in the driveway and waving. No one noticed they were being followed.

CHAPTER 39

They rode in the backseat of the cab, both men eating their burgers and onion rings, thinking how much better they would taste with an ice-cold beer. Both men lost in their thoughts about how they were going to break the news to their superiors and exactly what news would it be. How could they spin it so it didn't sound as bad as it was? Number 1 looked sick to his stomach, knowing he would be the one who had to make the call. Number 2 smiled knowingly. He didn't have to.

The cabbie pulled up in front of their hotel, and as he stepped on the brakes, he yelled. "Whoa, horsey!" and acted like he was pulling back on the reigns. "This is the last stop for the stagecoach. Everybody off!" The cabbie continued with a laugh.

"Fuck you very much!" Number 1 said, walking away without paying and flashing his Secret Service ID. "That was official business partner."

Number 2 laughed and gave the cabbie a good look at his middle finger sticking up, "You're number one!" He laughed again. "That's your tip!" They both strolled into the hotel, knowing the first thing they were going to do was ditch their rodeo outfits and go back to the suits they were used to wearing.

CHAPTER 40

Cliff started down the street that led to Frank's basement and came to a slow roll then decided against it. They would give him more time, and besides, they had had enough excitement for one day already. A beer and a bong hit is what he needed, they needed, and he knew that they both were at Freddie's dad's house.

The car came to a stop along the curb out in front of Freddie's house. They always parked in the street because a basketball game could break out at any time, and a car would only get in the way. The three of them made a beeline for Freddie's bedroom where the bong awaited them. Oh how badly they needed to get stoned. The beer could come later, once the cottonmouth settled in. Three bong hits each, and they were standing in front of the refrigerator, drawing a pitcher of beer to take outside with them. Freddie grabbed the ladder and wrenches to take down the old broken backboard. Cliff and Lee tore open the box holding the new rim and backboard, the next victim of the ensuing slam dunk assault.

Two pitchers later, the new hoop was up, and they stood in the driveway, stoned and dribbling the basketball. The ball was old and slick, and they wondered why they hadn't bought a new one the other day. Half drunk and half baked, they all went through the motions of playing b ball. But it was clear they had the events of the day in the front of their minds.

"So what do you guys make of all that shit that happened today and what Jenny was talking about?" Cliff finally asked.

"Shit, Cliff. I don't know. Even if you believed in coincidences, that would still be a butt load of 'em," Freddie replied.

Lee sat back, drinking beer and listening to his friends volley back and forth. He had seen this go on many times before, and it was a way for them to get confirmation, or not, of what was going on in their heads. It was always interesting to watch.

"Those suits in the trunk, those trip me out along with the rental car. There can't be too many reasons why somebody would be so anxious to gamble off their rental car, right?"

"Fuck, Cliff. The only idea I have is the same ones you do. What's your take on it?" Freddie was trying to spin this conversation so he could ask the questions because he knew he had no answers, only guesses.

"Fuck if I know!" Cliff said. "I suppose it could be something to do with our fishing trip, but how could that be? We haven't told anybody about it." Cliff then realized Freddie had pulled off his trick of turning around the conversation on him, and that only meant one thing, Freddie had more questions than answers, which made him just like himself, and that was something that very rarely happened. One of them seemed to have some clarity when the other did not. "I really don't know what to think. Jenny is usually pretty sharp, so it's hard to dismiss what she says. Besides, she's the one with fresh eyes on the situation," Cliff finished.

They both drank another beer with Lee since he looked like the only one with the best answers so far. This seemed to put a worry inside of Lee. His friends always seem to figure out the answers to all of their situations.

They sat on the steps of the front porch in silence, sipping their beer together. When the glasses and the pitcher were empty, Freddie went inside to draw another pitcher from the tap.

Freddie once again joined his friends on the front steps, filling glasses from the fresh pitcher and quickly noticing that their attention was focused on the sports car parked on the street. At least that was what his first thought it was and then he saw what it really was. His neighbor from across the street was walking in their direction, wearing his customary tie-dyed T-shirt and cutoff jeans shorts that had an inch and a half of fray at the bottom of them.

"What's up?" Freddie asked him, not knowing how to address him but knew that Crazy Harry, as they called him, probably was not the way. Right away, Freddie noticed that his neighbor looked different, not, so crazy in the eyes as he remembered him from past events in the neighborhood. Perhaps he was having another moment of clarity.

Crazy Harry started right in. "You don't know what you've gotten yourselves into, do you?" Not pausing for answers to his questions. "Did you know they are after you? What did you do? Do you know that they won't go away until they get what they want? They are watching you! I can prove it to you!" All at once, he turned at the end of the driveway and sprinted in his bare feet down the middle of the asphalt road and through the four-way stop intersection, almost getting hit by a car. He continued sprinting toward a metallic light blue 4Runner parked halfway down the block. All at once, the 4Runner took off in reverse and backed into a driveway a couple of houses further away and then sped off down the road away from him. All three stood there in the driveway, not believing their eyes, and wondering how much weird shit could anyone pack into one day.

Breathing heavily, Crazy Harry returned from down the street, stopped at the end of the driveway, and said, "I told you, didn't I?" He then turned and walked toward his house, stopping again in the middle of the street. "Those guys want their car back!" as he nodded in the direction of the red Austin Martin parked in front of the house. "Not those two you got it from, but the people who really own it!"

The three of them stood paralyzed in the driveway with their mouths hanging wide open. The basketball bounced and then rolled out into the street. No one chased after it. The rim and backboard would live to see another day. They were all on their way to the bong and could not get there fast enough.

CHAPTER 41

"Check it out." Freddie started in. "I think I am gonna stay here at my dad's tonight. If I stay in town, I can check in with Frank first thing in the morning to see about the Discs. I also want to pick Jenny's brain about those two guys from the jet," he continued. "I don't know what you want to do about that car out front. Personally, I would have some fun driving the shit out of it and then park it at the Hertz Rent-A-Car. Dean should have the new tires and wheels on the Challenger. You guys could go by the shop and pick it up or leave it there and pick up the red racer. Depends on what you want to explain to your mother, Cliff, but lying low right now might be the best idea. I don't know about you, but that Crazy Harry shit has got me tripping."

"Yeah, you are probably right. Whatever is on those discs must be important," Cliff said.

"No shit, Sherlock! We found them with thirty million dollars! Of course, they are important!"

"I think we should wait another thirty minutes before taking off, so it's dark enough to tell if anybody is following us once we reach the country roads."

"That's a good idea. Here, you want a hit off this before I put it away? Sorry about freaking out on you for a second there, but this whole thing has really got me going now. I am thinking we may be in way over our heads on this one, fellas."

"I'll take a hit," Lee spoke up. "Maybe more than one!"

"Shit, that's twice today the big man has had the best idea. You going for some kind of record?" said Cliff and then they all laughed.

They sat there in silence, drinking beer and passing around the bong. As soon as dark started marking the end of the day, they slipped out of town, and no lights followed.

CHAPTER 42

Freddie had told his friends that he was going to go see Frank in the morning, but he had no intentions of waiting that long. Fifteen or twenty minutes after they left, he was on his bike, pedaling the few blocks to Frank's house.

Frank was startled by the knock on this basement door. Nobody ever knocked.

"Come on in. It's open," Frank yelled.

"What's up?" Freddie asked while stepping inside, closing and locking the door.

"Not much where are the other two stooges?"

"You're a real funny guy, not!' Freddie shot back. "Up on the hill by now, I suppose. It's just me tonight."

"Well, aren't I the lucky one."

"I don't know. Maybe I'm the lucky guy. I didn't walk in on you cleaning your monitor." Freddie laughed.

"Funny guy!" Frank laughed too.

"I know you're here about the discs, and I have to admit to you I am pretty much stumped. My next plan, which you are just in time for, is to put them into the Disc drive while I am connected to the Internet and see if Windows can find me a program to open them with. It's a long shot, but it's all we got."

"Yes, I am here for that, and a little something else I need your help with."

"What is it now?" Frank said, sounding annoyed.

"Don't get all pissy, Frank. This is going to be an easy one for you."

"Okay, but first things first. Hand me that disc."

"This is going to be really cool," said Frank beaming with excitement. "I have a buddy at intel that gave me a backdoor way into their computer mainframe. From there, was able to hack into the Federal Governments System. . ."

"Jesus Christ, Frank!" Freddie yelled. "Are you fucking serious? I don't want to hear any more of this shit! Don't make me a witness to espionage! What the fuck is wrong with you?"

Freddie slipped the Disc off of the table and handed it to Frank, who already had the tray to his Disc drive open.

"Let me get this started and then we can deal with your other problem while the internet is finding us the program to open these babies up."

Frank dropped it into the tray, closed the drive, and started his search. The hard drive clicked, the Disc drive spun, and the computer fans whirled. Before Frank could stand up from his chair, a message flashed onto his monitor.

"What the fuck!" Frank yelled.

With the blink of an eye, the monitor went blank, and the whirling and clicking of Frank's computer came to a halt, and the lights on the front of his computer went black.

"What's wrong? What happened? Did I accidently pull a cord?" Freddie asked.

"No, nothing like that happened, but I think your little disc's just fucked up my system."

"What do you mean?"

"What I mean is that your fucking discs fucked up my system. Shut it down completely!"

"How is that possible? Is that possible?"

"It sure as fuck looks like it. My whole system has gone completely dead!"

"Shit, Frank. I don't know what to say," Freddie said. Though he did know little about what to say, he could tell him about all of the weird shit that had happened that day and how that was just another thing in a long string of things that was hard to explain.

"All I know is that the screen flashed a message and then everything went dead!"

"Message? What message?"

"The screen flashed, 'These discs are protected as a matter of National Security. Your system will now shut down,' then everything went dead. Just like that," Frank said as he snapped his fingers. "That tower was worth a thousand dollars! Who the fuck is going to pay for that?" Frank asked.

"Here, buddy," Freddie said as he reached into his pocket and pulled out three grand. Here are two. I will pay for the upgrade, but you have to help me with one more thing."

"As long as it doesn't involve these fucking discs, I will do whatever you want," Frank replied, snatching up the two grand from Freddie's hand, already dreaming about how nice of a system he could build with two grand.

"Cool! This will only take us a couple of minutes, I promise," Freddie said as he walked over to one of Franks work benches and told him what he needed.

CHAPTER 43

Back in Washington DC, in the offices of the Secret Service, along the wall that held the computer system and monitors for the office, a light flashed brightly and constantly while a buzzer buzzed loudly and a GPS location was printed out and then pulled by hand from the printer. Somewhere in the world, somebody had put in one of the missing discs into their computer, and those discs, by design, sent a signal directly to the main headquarters of the Secret Service and disclosed the location of that signal. Also by design, the agents knew that the system used would be rendered useless by the time they received the signal.

Back in Hillsboro, Oregon, not far from where the signal originated, the phone inside Smith's Number 1 hotel room rang and orders were given and orders were received. Number 1 knocked on Number 2's door.

"We have orders that must be carried out tonight, so put that thing away and meet me in the hall in ten minutes. The cab is already on the way," said Number 1.

"Are you fucking crazy?" Number 2 said as he appeared from his room. "We can't do a mission from a cab!"

"No shit!" Number 1 replied while looking Number 2 up and down. "Why in the fuck are you still wearing that fucking cowboy outfit?"

"I kinda like 'em, partner."

"Don't be starting that shit with me! Come on. Let's go. The cab will be here soon."

They went downstairs and jumped in the cab waiting for them by the front entrance of the hotel. Right away he recognized them.

"Don't you two make a cute couple," said the cabbie.

"Just shut up and drive!" replied Number 1. Then he tossed him the address he had written down on the piece of scrap paper. "I assume you can read?" was the last thing said for the remainder of the cab ride.

The cabbie hit the gas, pulled away from the hotel breaking every speed limit along his way, wanting nothing more than to get the asshole out of his cab. Watching in his mirrors along the way, he noticed that they had picked up a tail since leaving the hotel. He thought about letting them know, but then thought, Fuck them. They will probably stiff him on the ride anyway, so he directed his attention forward, on the road, and drove along in silence.

Number 1 and Number 2 never considered that anyone would follow them, so neither of them noticed the Toyota 4Runner with tinted windows following their every move.

CHAPTER 44

The cab pulled into the hidden driveway of the makeshift army base. There was no one manning the front gate. As Number 1 pushed the intercom button, they could see a surveillance camera turn their way.

"It's Smith. You are expecting us."

"Sure am, ladies. Pull into the right and park. I will be right out to meet you with the keys to your new ride."

When Colonel North said "new ride." They instantly thought he meant new car. What he really meant was new to them, not in age. So when the cab driver parked next to the 1970 Dodge Dart, they had no clue they were sitting next to their new ride.

"Here's your keys, ladies. You may want to warm her up a bit before you take off. She's been sitting for a while. Oh yeah, every fifty miles or so, you will need to add oil to her. She tends to burn more and more every day. Your superior officer said you wouldn't need it for very long, so I think she will hold out for ya, the colonel finished with a sarcastic laugh and then turned, walking away from them, and with his back turned, he waved good-bye and raised his middle finger.

"You a cocksucker, North!" yelled Number 1.

"Well, I was a dumb fuck before, so it sounds like I am moving up!" North laughed again. "See that nice new Cadillac parked right next to you? That's the rental car I picked up for you two clowns today, and it's the one I will be driving around. You might want to be careful who you call a dumb fuck, Smith. You never know who you might need a favor from!" North yelled almost from his office door. "And you two really do make a cute couple!"

"Fuck you, North!" Smith Number 1 yelled, but it was too late. North was already inside his office with his door closed. It was a quiet night, and the Smiths could hear the cabbie laughing all the way out of the front gate.

"Fuck you too!" They hopped into their new ride and sat there for a minute, waiting for it to warm up. Each man were thinking to themselves that this was going to be a long night.

CHAPTER 45

Frank and Freddie fiddled around in Frank's basement for another hour or two until they finally found everything Freddie needed and then spent the next twenty minutes assembling the parts. Once Freddie was satisfied, he packed up his backpack and pushed his bike toward the door.

"Are you going to tell me what kind of bullshit you have gotten yourself into or what?" Frank asked as Freddie headed out the door and started his way up the steps from his basement.

"Someday, Frank. I will tell you someday," Freddie replied as he turned back toward Frank and waved good-bye to him. Freddie might have told him right then and there if he knew that it would be the last he would ever see Frank, at least see him alive.

"Well, be careful," Frank yelled as Freddie hopped on his bike and pedaled away into the night.

"Always am!" Freddie yelled back. "Always am!"

Sitting in the shadows of a big corkscrew willow tree sat a 1970 faded red Dodge Dart with two men ducking down inside the front seat as a kid on his bike rode past, wearing his Adidas backpack.

"This must be the right place because I swear that was one of those fucking little brats that beat us in that car race earlier today," said Number 2. "I wonder why he is riding a bike instead of driving around the car they took from us today," he continued.

"I don't know," replied Number 1. "But if we weren't under orders to do this thing first, I would jump out and put a bullet in his skull right now!"

"Let's do this one thing first. We will have time later to get even with those little bastards!"

The Smiths waited until he pedaled out of sight and then quietly exited the car, leaving the doors slightly ajar so as not to make any noise. As they snuck down to Frank's basement, they didn't notice the Toyota 4Runner pull out and do a 180 then follow the kid on his bike.

Reaching the bottom of the stairs to Frank's basement, Smith Number 1 tried the doorknob to the house and found it wasn't locked. Both men pulled out their new service pistols, screwed on silencers they had been issued for this mission. Number 1 threw the door open wide, and both men stepped into the basement and were quickly upon the kid, the only person inside the basement. Once they had him fully detained, they explained why they were here and what it was that they wanted.

Having no choice in the matter, Frank quickly told them where they could find the disc. After all, they told him he would live and that they only wanted the discs. Frank had hoped that they were telling the truth. It became obvious, once they got the discs in their possession, that they were not going to be leaving any witnesses.

They call them silencers, but they still made some noise. As soon as Frank gave them directions to where the boys would be, Smith Number 1 pulled his trigger. His gun made a pffft, pffft sound that was only heard by the men in the basement. As the Smiths left, holding the prize, they left Frank sitting in his computer chair like he did most of every day, looking like he was once again cleaning his monitor. But a closer look told the real story. Frank was dead.

The two men sat in their 4Runner, following and watching as the kid turned into the driveway and rode his bike through the gate opening of the fence that ran along the side of the house. Once through the gate and off his bike, the sliding glass door was drawn open, and Freddie stepped inside to see Jenny eating ice cream and wearing her pajamas. It was the same house they saw the kids at earlier that day, only earlier, they were cruising around in a ninety-thousand-dollar sports car. The men eased back in their seats and took turns watching, waiting for something to happen and if it did one would awaken the other so that the quest to find their bosses missing thirty million dollars could continue.

Number 1 started the car as soon as Number 2 finished pouring another quart of oil into the old Dodge Dart. If he had a chance, he would also put a bullet into that cocksucker North's head for giving them the old, piece-of-shit car to go do a hit.

CHAPTER 46

As Jenny sat and listened Freddie talked, telling her everything, at least everything that happened earlier that day. Freddie had made a promise to his friends, and he would keep that promise even if there was pussy on the line. Jenny took in everything he told her, sometimes having him back up a bit to clarify one thing or another.

When Freddie finished, Jenny began and told him everything she had learned from her mother, who had told Jenny what her boyfriend had seen and heard at the airport where he worked, cleaning out planes and putting fuel in them for their next flights.

Once all of the pieces were out on the table, they both worked at fitting them together. This is where these two friends really shined. Give them a certain amount of facts and time to discuss them, and they could paint a picture that was clear to see. Assembling the parts, using information from both female and male points of view, they had never met a situation that they couldn't predict.

Jenny began to lay out the finishing touches of her and his take on things. As she did, concern began to grow on Freddie's face.

"Frank!" Freddie yelled. "Where is your phone? I need to call Frank now!"

Jenny handed him the phone and frantically dialed Frank's number. Finally, it began to ring. On the fourth ring, Freddie could hear the receiver being picked up at the other end.

"Frank, this is Freddie. Listen to me and listen good. I don't have much time to tell you and you much trust me and do what I tell you without any questions. It is a matter of life and death!"

As Freddie talked on, Jenny and Frank listened to Freddie. He explained everything that happened earlier that day and how men had been following them all over town. He told Frank about the car race and the clothes they found in the car and also about the goings on at the airport. Freddie laid it all on the line and then finished with, "You must get the fuck out of your basement now, Frank! Do it now!"

There was silence at the other end of the line and then a voice said, "It's too late. He's already dead," and then the line went dead.

Smith Number 1 waited about ten seconds then picked up the receiver, dialed in his special code, and requested a trace on the last number that called the phone. Within a minute, he had an address in hand.

CHAPTER 47

Freddie hung up the phone then sank in against the back of the couch and waited for Jenny to ask him what he heard on the phone, hoping that in time, the answer he had to give her would change. Finally, before she could say a word, he blurted it out, "Franks dead! The man on the phone said we were too late, that Frank's was already dead!"

Tears welled up in both their eyes. Freddie dialed up Lisa's number, but there was no answer. He tried again and again with the same results.

"I've got to get up on the hill and warn Lee and Cliff," Freddie said as he put on his backpack and headed toward the sliding glass door.

"I want to go with you," Jenny said.

"No, you stay here where it is safe and try calling Lisa's phone until somebody answers. If they do, tell Lisa to get Cliff on the line. Cliff will know what to do," Freddie said, going out the door. "It will take me a good thirty–forty minutes to get up there."

Jenny hugged him, kissed his cheek, and told him to be careful. He looked deep into her eyes and then turned and left out the door without saying another word. Freddie gave his bike a running push and jumped onto the seat and took off across Jenny's mom's front lawn and pedaled faster than he ever pedaled before.

Inside, Jenny dialed Lisa's number again and again, trying to will her into answering the phone.

Outside, both men, still awake, sitting in the 4Runner watched as the kid with the backpack pushed his bike across the front lawn before jumping on and pedaling down the street. As he did, the old Dodge Dart fell in behind him and followed the bike at a safe distance.

The two men in the 4Runner would wait there for their chance. They had their orders and would not be caught chasing their tails like their Secret Service counterparts.

Inside, Jenny took a break from dialing Lisa's number to tack postage to the front of the package Freddie had asked her to mail for him. Reading the address, *Washington Post*, care of reporter, Michael Johnson. Jenny began to wonder what might be in the envelope marked for a newspaper columnist on the other side of the country. Then after thinking about it, she thought it best to forget about it, judging by the chain of recent events, and went back to dialing Lisa's number still with no luck.

Outside, both men noticed the time on the clock showing on the dash of the Toyota. The sun would be coming up soon, and soon after that would come their moment to act.

CHAPTER 48

Of course, Lee and Cliff would not listen to his advice to ditch the little red Austin Martin sports car, and when he finally reached the barn, it was right where he could have predicted it would be, under a heavy tarp, stashed next to the old truck waiting for his mom to find the next time she came out to feed the cows or water the goat. If Cliff thought it would be hard to explain to his mother before Freddie wondered how hard it would be now. Freddie was already curious how they explained the Dodge Challenger that now sat in the middle of the front lawn between Lisa's house and the guest house. That would certainly make for an interesting discussion in the not too distant future.

As Freddie dipped into the barn, he noticed that the suns glow had started to break free over the eastern horizon. The bright yellow-and-orange sky was almost blinding if he was to stare too long. When you closed your eyes, you could still see the purplish colored light in your mind.

Freddie would have to hurry in order to finish the work he had in front of him and still have time to wake Lisa and warn her off the hill before daybreak then call Jenny to let her know that he made it there safe and to slap Lee and Cliff out of their drunken slumber before the day got late.

Up in the loft, he dug out the dry bags so he could stash them under the barn and connect them to a warning signal, a booby trap. Dragging the bags out of the loft and lifting the floorboards, he stuck a special package into the bags for the person, other than them, to find. It was sort of a surprise package. As he lifted the floorboards and hefted the bags into place, Freddie saw a shadow flash out of the corner of his eye. He looked up, and standing in the sunlight, coming through the door was Cliff.

"What the fuck are you doing?" he asked.

"What the fuck does it look like I'm doing?' Freddie shot back. "I will give you all of the details in a minute, but first help me stuff the bags under here and set the alarm and booby trap," Freddie continued.

"Have you lost your fucking mind?"

"No, I haven't, and I will explain myself, just fucking help me, please!"

"Okay, just quit trippin'."

"Besides, you're asking me if I've lost my mind when you have a ninety-thousand-dollar sports car stashed under a tarp in your barn. What's your mom gonna say?"

"Don't go worrying about me. How did you cut yourself?" Cliff asked, pointing to the blood trail that was running down the side of his neck and building a growing stain on his shirt.

"I don't know. It must been one of those bags. Those fuckers are heavy."

"Okay, and the dirty smudge on your face? It kinda matches the clean spot on my dad's coolers."

"I was going to hide the bags in them, but they weren't big enough. Is this twenty questions or are you going to help?"

"A little of both, I guess."

Working together, they stuffed both bags full of money under the trap door of the barn and then set the booby trap.

Cliff listened while Freddie explained what had happened during the past eight–ten hours, more than once saying the word "unbelievable" out loud. As Freddie began to wrap up his narrative they both walked toward the main house. Once they entered, Freddie went straight for the phone to call Jenny, and Cliff went upstairs to wake his mother.

Lee walked into the main house, still rubbing his eyes awake, but also holding the day's first beer in his hand.

"What's going on, fellas?" Lisa asked.

The thought of having to repeat the whole story again before drinking a beer sounded to him as being impossible, so Freddie told Lee to grab him a beer and that he would meet him in the guest house and give him all the details and that he may as well load the bong too.

Freddie reached Jenny on the second ring of the phone. He told her that he had made it onto the hill without incident, and she told him that her mother had just left for work and that she also had the extra postage it would take to mail his package. She assured him that his package was on its way. Freddie thanked her, and she told him to be careful as they hung up the phone.

Cliff hurried his mother down the stairs and out of the house and to her car, pressing her as she went on protesting a little. If it were not for the seriousness in his voice, she would have been certain the three kids were up to something. Lisa climbed in her car, started it up, and headed down Bishop Road. She didn't even notice the old Dodge Dart cross her path as she turned onto Helvetia Road and started her way to town. To where, she didn't know, just away from the hill.

CHAPTER 49

Jenny stood in the kitchen, drinking her morning coffee after saying good-bye to her mother, who was now on her way to the post office and then go on to work for the day. Jenny was on her way to the phone to try Lisa's number again when the phone started to ring. She picked up on the second ring and was relieved to hear it was Freddie on the other end. He informed her that all was fine. He got there okay, and that Cliff was waking his mother up as they speak, and that she would soon be leaving the hill. Everyone was safe and sound.

Jenny said her good-byes, told him to be careful, and then hung up the phone. She turned to go upstairs to take her morning shower, only to see two big, scary-looking Columbians standing in her kitchen, pointing guns at her. There was no place to run, and no place to hide. In her head, she wished she had left with Freddie. Little did she know that she would be seeing him soon, that her wish was about to be granted.

CHAPTER 50

Freddie, Lee, and Cliff all met back up in the guest house after Lisa was safe and off of the hill and the call to Jenny had been made. Freddie had been very busy all night and needed a minute or two to rest, drink a beer, and down a couple of bong hits. His two friends waited patiently for him to get himself into the state of mind that he needed to begin his story.

They both listened intently. Lee for the first time, and Cliff for the second. Even the second time around, the story sounded like something from the silver screen or from one of those made-up fiction books from the school library. It took close to an hour, three beers, and the occasional bong hit to get the story out and get it out straight.

The part where their friend was said to be dead (no confirmation as of yet) and with the passing of all of the events of the previous day, it all wasn't that hard to believe. The story wrapped up with the stashing of the money then a trip to the main house to wake Lisa and call Jenny. It was also the place where Lee walked into the house half awake and halfway through his first beer of the day. So they sat there in silence, just looking at each other, each thinking about what should be their next move.

How in the hell could a fishing trip a mere four days ago had led them to this point, seemingly a life-and-death situation. They were just three kids looking forward to a time of fun in the sun during summer break. Now they all wondered if they would still be alive to see today's sun set in the west.

That was the spot where Cliff had always come through in the past. Cliff would come up with a plan that would lead all out of harm's way. As his friends looked to him to one more time save their asses, all he could do was stare back in silence. This time, he had no answers.

Lee walked to the kitchen, opened the fridge, and pulled out three more beers, popped the tops then handed them to his friends, a typical Lee move. When in doubt, drink another beer. Since he was the only one with any answers at all, they clanged them together and they all said, "Cheers" then took a good long pull of their beers. Silence once again followed.

CHAPTER 51

Back in town, Jenny was being lead at gunpoint to the 4Runner awaiting them at the curb. Still dressed in nothing but her pajamas and slippers. They had her climb into the passenger seat to give directions to her friend's house. It was also the easiest way to hold her at gunpoint. Even though she wasn't one of those three boys they had watched time after time, somehow escaping harm's way at the expense of the Secret Service. Mistakes like that would mean a death sentence from their boss. They would take no chances.

As Jenny gave directions, they followed them, passing through what had become familiar territory for the past few days when they first picked up the trail of hundred dollar bills, leading them out to the country.

Passing the tavern and then turning onto Bishop Road and into new territory, they reminded her that any false direction would lead her to her death.

She led; they followed. All she could think about was what they would do once they reached their destination. Could it be that even the correct directions could lead her to her death? Only time would tell.

CHAPTER 52

The old Dodge Dart was parked at the spot in the road where Bishop Road ended and the driveway to Cliff's house began. Driving down it, they would have a straightaway followed by a sweeping right hand turn, making a full 90 degree angle, and set them on the final straightaway up to the house's detached garage and the concrete basketball court that made up the entrance to the barn. To get to the main house, they had to follow the narrow concrete path that led to the wooden front porch and to the front door of the house.

The first stretch of driveway skirted the edge of the tall wooded area that stretched its way toward the back of the big, withered grey wooden barn. If it was a year old, it was a hundred, and was still being used. At least the cows and goat didn't mind and the chickens didn't care because they had a coupe of their own and had free reign of the front yard.

The eastern side of the driveway gave way to endless fields of yellow hay, and beyond it stood the first and closest neighbor's house. Close might not be the best word to describe the distance between the two houses, for it was anything but close. Privacy was definitely assured.

Due to the lay of the land, a car of any sort would have a tough time sneaking up on the place, but sneaking up on foot was a whole different story.

That's exactly how the two Smiths proceeded with their assault on the property. They would have been quite a sight if anyone had seen them. One in a seersucker suit and the other one dressed like a rodeo cowboy.

Quietly and fairly quickly, they were able to walk along the edge of the woods and come out around the back of the barn. The two of them could have made better time if it wasn't for the thoughts they had. It seemed that no matter what they did, it never turned out anyway other than wrong. It seemed like a clear case of Murphy's Law. If it could go wrong, it would. Caution was their word of the day.

Number 2 made it to the back of the barn first, but Number 1 was right behind him. Number 2 had made better time due to his cowboy boots being better suited for the patch of cow shit they had to wade through. Number 1 didn't care he would never wear a cowboy outfit ever again.

Both men ducked through the fence that kept the cows out of the front part of the barn and soon found themselves on the sturdy ground that made up the barn's floor. Walking over toward the old truck, Number 1 pulled on the heavy tarp next to the truck and uncovered the sports car they had lost in the race not so long ago. Both men smiled, thinking about how they would be driving out of here in the shiny red Austin Martin and also how much fun it was going to be, making the call to North, telling him where he could find his old Dodge Dart. And that when he found it, he could go ahead and shove it up his ass!

Both Smiths walked to the big sliding doors that served as the entrance to the barn for trucks with hay or any other farm vehicle could pull right in. As Smith Number 2 stepped forward behind Number 1, a flash of yellow from between the cracks of the boards that made up the barn's floor caught his eye. Tapping Number 1's shoulder and pointing toward the ground, they both could now see the two yellow dry bags that they so desperately wanted to find.

They both reached down to lift up the trap door to access the bags, and when they did, it set off a chain reaction. Mr. Murphy had showed up again.

The trap door pulled up, the gate came down, and the bell clanged loudly. The next thing they saw was a pissed-off billy goat charging at them on his hind legs and then crashing down upon them, skull to skull. It was a two-hit fight—the goat hit them, and they hit the floor.

CHAPTER 53

All three boys were brought out of their daydreams and drunkenness, first by the clanging of the bell; second, the baying of the goat; and third; the cracking of either a skull against skull or a skull against the barn's wooden floor. Either way, the pop was loud and sounded very painful.

Freddie was the fastest and got there first. Cliff followed second, and Lee brought up the rear. In any order it wouldn't matter because they all knew there was a pissed-off billy goat on the loose behind those barn doors, so approaching with caution was their first concern.

They eased the barn door open slowly, giving the goat a way to escape, and making the coast clear to enter the barn. The goat immediately ran out the door to freedom, and started chasing chickens around the front yard, thus keeping him busy, so they stepped slowly into the barn.

There on the barn floor lay the two men from the tavern and the car race, only now one was wearing a suit and the other was still dressed for a Boot Leg clothing ad. But both were knocked out cold. Minutes later, after first tying their hands and feet together, Cliff doused them with a bucketful of water from the cow trough to bring them back around and awake.

"You fellas sure seem to get around," Cliff said. "You mind telling me what the fuck you're doing in my barn, and why you are fuckin with my goat? I have a mind to nail your nuts to a stump and push you over backward!" Cliff continued.

For the moment, both Smiths were exercising their rights to remain silent. What they failed to recognize was that those rights only apply to those who are being arrested.

"That's fine. You two can keep quiet if you want to, or I can bring billy back in here, and you fellas can work it out with him!" Freddie laughed. "It's all up to you, fellas, so do whatever you want!"

Neither one said a word; a few minutes passed until Cliff made a move to go get the goat back into the barn.

"You kids are making a huge mistake!" cried Number 1.

"That's kinda funny, coming from a guy that's just been caught red-handed in another man's barn," Cliff answered back.

"At first glance, it may appear that way, but we work for the Secret Service, and back up is on the way," Number 1 shot back.

"That's funny because I was about to guess that you guys made up two fifths of the Village People, and that the other three were on their way," Freddie said, and all three laughed.

"Everybody in this fuckin town thinks they are comedians, don't they?"

"You two kinda lend yourselves to being made fun of," Cliff responded.

Lee reached inside of Number 1 and pulled out his ID from his wallet. "I'll be damned if it doesn't say Secret Service," he said. "And there is a little badge in here too."

"Hell, anybody could make one of those, and if this is the way our Secret Service operates, it's no wonder how all of those conspiracy theories seem to gravitate around them," Cliff said. "You two seem to be one big mistake after another just waiting to happen."

"Save us the speech, kid" Number 1 said. "I order you to cut us loose!" Number 1 yelled.

"Yeah, well I order you to go fuck yourselves! If you haven't noticed yet, you're not really in a position to be given out orders," Cliff replied. "Is he always this big of a prick?" Cliff asked Number 2 while nodding his head at Number 1.

Number 2 only sat there then he finally said, "I better take the fifth on that one."

"If you're Secret Service then why are you here?" Cliff asked.

"You know damn well why we are here!"

"The money or the discs or both?"

"Mostly the discs, but the money too. Only it belongs to somebody you don't want to be fuckin with."

"The discs aren't in those bags any more. I have them right here!" Freddy said, holding up his backpack." He continued, "You know what, Lee, this one here sounds like the motherfucker that claims to have killed Frank last night."

The three boys huddled around each other, trying to decide what they were going to do next, wondering if there was a way out of the mess where they could keep the money. At the moment, things didn't look good.

CHAPTER 54

At the bottom of the driveway, the Toyota 4runner pulled in behind the old Dodge Dart and came to a stop.

"Which house is your friend's?" They asked Jenny.

"That one," Jenny pointed to the one on top of the hill.

Both men walked behind Jenny and followed her straight up the middle of the driveway. Jenny knew that doing it this way would make it easy for her friends to see them walking up the driveway toward the house. Even if they did see them. she had serious doubts there was anything anybody could do about it.

They walked far enough up the driveway to be next to the guest house and close enough to hear people talking inside of the barn. From the conversation, they could make out that it sounded like the kids were issuing orders to the men. 'Could they have gotten the drop on them again?' asked one of the Columbians, grabbing Jenny around the neck and pointing his pistol up against the side of her head. They then slowly approached the front of the barn.

One Columbian held the gun to Jenny's head while the other one slid the barn door wide open. It was easy to see that they were the only ones holding any guns and, therefore, took total control of the situation.

"Everybody hold your hands up where I can see them and keep them there!" the Columbian holding the gun to Jenny's head yelled. "I'm only going to say this once, and if I don't get what I want, I am going to put a bullet in this pretty lady's head. Does everybody understand?"

Not a soul said a word in response. "Good, then I want the two bags of money, and I want them placed in the trunk of that fancy little red sports car. Now!"

Freddie reached down under the barn with Lee and lifted the bags up. Then Lee placed them both into the truck of the Austin Martin.

"Now hand me the fucking keys, and don't try none of your tricky stuff you've been using on those two. If you do, the girl gets it!"

Lee slowly handed him the keys to the sports car. It was his turn to drive it next, so he had the keys in his pocket. Lee said, "This is bullshit!" as he gave away the car and his turn to drive it all in one motion.

Holding Jenny by the neck still, the Columbians sidestepped their way to the car, keeping a close eye on the three kids.

"You have your money, now give us the girl!" Freddie said. "You don't need her anymore!"

The Columbian carefully opened the passenger side door, and just before sitting down, shoved Jenny forward into Freddie's waiting arms. Then seconds later, they were sending up a big cloud of dust and heading off the dirt driveway and flying down Bishop Road.

Jenny was half laughing and half crying with her arms wrapped tightly around Freddie shoulders. "You sure know how to show a girl a good time!" Jenny said, laughing. Freddie laughed with her as he also returned her hug.

Jenny stepped back a little after their hug and then asked the three of them, "How much money did you guys just give up to get me back?"

Cliff, Lee, and Freddie stared at each other, and in unison said, "Thirty million dollars. Thirty million dollars," saying it twice for they could hardly believe the words coming out of their mouths.

CHAPTER 55

The four kids stood there on the concrete basketball court/entry to the barn, hugging each other and laughing and being happy they were still alive. Knowing that all of that was behind them and the bad guys with the guns were down the road and racing in the other direction.

"Are you punks gonna untie us?" Number 1 yelled.

During all the excitement, they had forgotten all about the two men they still kept tied up in the barn.

"I really don't know how to answer that question yet," Cliff said. "I think it may take a couple of beers and maybe a bong hit or two before I can answer you."

All four of them turned toward the guest house and started to walk. As they walked, they heard the *whomp, whomp, whomp* sound of a helicopter getting closer and closer. In a flash, the Dodge Challenger was strafed by 50 caliber gunshots and burst into flames. Moments later, three choppers appeared from the north. One of them had the Presidential seal on the side, and the other two they recognized as Apache gunships like the ones they had seen at last year's air show. The first one landed while the other two hovered in the air a short distance away.

The door fell open, revealing a set of stairs, and two men dressed in military uniforms stepped off of the chopper and ran past the kids and into the barn. They went straight to the Smiths. They cut the bindings from their wrist and ankles then helped them to their feet and escorted them onto the helicopter. The two men and the four kids all exchanged dirty looks with one another as they passed each other on their way to the chopper. Lee decided to flash them the middle finger of both hands, providing them with his idea of an affectionate good-bye.

No sooner had they stepped up into the huge chopper then a single man stepped off and sauntered over to them. All of them knew right away that it was the President himself. He was a big man, bigger in real life than he was on the TV, and that was saying a lot. His jet black hair was parted down the side and meticulously combed over to the other. Not a hair was out of place. Jenny uttered the word, "Damn." And from past episodes, the three boys took it to mean he was a handsome man. As the chopper blades continued to rotate, stirring up some wind, not a hair on his head dared to step out of place.

The President talked and they listened. It was obvious that he expecting nothing else. His presence was mesmerizing, and the kids stood there, almost paralyzed. It was like a character from an old cowboy movie stepped out of the silver screen and walked up to them. They could swear he was ten feet tall.

"I want to thank you kids for taking such good care of my Discs for me, but now is the time for me to take possession of them. I am sure you can appreciate that fact and are probably more than happy to be rid of them," the President said, and they listened afraid to say a word.

Freddie lifted the Adidas backpack that was in his hand up toward the President without making a sound. As the big man grabbed hold of the backpack, he began to speak again, and all four, still in a trance, listened.

"These discs are a matter of national security, kids. Everything you have seen, heard, or experienced in the past four days is classified top secret and, if talked about, will be denied," he said. "Do you understand?" he asked.

All they could do was nod their heads, indicating that, yes, they got the message loud and clear.

"Thanks again," the President said as he spun around on his heels, walked away from them, and boarded the helicopter, and waved as the door to the chopper closed.

A short minute later, the four kids were alone on top of the hill, still looking skyward with their mouths open in amazement. Gone was the sound of the choppers, and in fact, there was nothing short of pure silence all around them.

"I will grab the beers!" Lee said, breaking the deafening silence.

"I will pack the bong!" Cliff said, following the big man toward the guest house.

Jenny grabbed Freddie's hand, fingers interlaced, and then followed their two friends toward the guest house.

There they sat next to one another, drinking beer and smoking pot. Even Jenny, who never smoked pot, took a hit that day. It seemed like an eternity had passed by. The day's events were nothing less than unbelievable, and the past week was in itself surreal.

Once or twice, they attempted to talk about what had just happened, and each time they did, it only lead to more silence. There were not words to describe the feelings that were overtaking them or the scenes that kept running through their heads.

"We're outta here!" Freddie said as he broke the silence. "I'm gonna take Jenny home and then head to my dad's. I think I will stay there tonight or maybe the rest of the week. Call me or I will call you," he said to Cliff and Lee. Neither of them believed he would call anytime soon.

"How are you gonna get home? All of the cars have been taken or blown up," Cliff asked.

"I figured I would walk down the driveway and have my pick out of the 4Runner or that old, piece-of-shit Dodge. Maybe I will find keys in them. We all know those fucking idiots left them in their car." They all attempted a laugh, but nothing that didn't sound fake came out of their mouths. "Lee can have what's left over and give you a ride down to McCall's shop to pick up the red racer." Freddie continued, "At least we will have something left from our thirty million dollars.

Jenny spoke up, "What do you mean? You guys will always have me."

The three friends searched each other's eyes for the words to respond, but each pair of eyes were only filled with emptiness.

Freddie grabbed Jenny's hand and led her back down the gravel driveway she had walked up not so very long ago. Not a word was spoken during their walk to the 4Runner, its keys were still in the ignition, or during their lonely drive back into town.

A good-bye and a peck on the cheek was all Freddie got before Jenny stepped out of the 4Runner. For thirty million dollars, he was hoping for more. Freddie pointed the Toyota toward home, and when he got there, he parked it at the curb, went inside to take a shower, and went to bed. Maybe it was all just a dream.

CHAPTER 56

The little red sports car flew down the back country roads and then slowly pulled up to the security gate and punched in the code they were given by their American friends. Once opened, they pulled the car onto the small airfield that made up the Hillsboro Airport and darted in behind the hangar located toward the back of the runway.

It was if someone knew they were coming and that was most assuredly true. The hangar door slid open. They grabbed their only luggage, two yellow dry bags stuffed to the top with one hundred dollar bills. No sooner had they boarded the small Lear jet, they were rolling down the runway and then flying toward the Pacific Ocean, ascending toward cruising speed and altitude.

One of the Columbians grabbed a dry bag and began to dump it out for counting. Along with the bundles of fresh one hundred dollar bills rolled out a pipe bomb with an altimeter detonator attached to it. As the jet reached twenty-five feet, all you could hear were two Columbians saying in unison, "Oh shit!" And then the bomb exploded tearing a huge hole in the side of the aircraft. Raining down with the wreckage were one hundred dollar bills burning until they hit the water of the Pacific Ocean. Freddie's special package had been delivered and performed just as designed.

CHAPTER 57

Freddie woke around noon the next day and started it off with a morning bong hit. He stumbled, still half asleep, into the bathroom. Then window was partly open, and he could see right away that it was not a dream. There was the 4Runner still parked along the curb out in front of his house.

As Freddie got dressed, he found the two unopened shoe boxes from Three Stripe Sports that he had packed upstairs in what seemed like an eternity ago but was really only a week. He pulled the laces tight on his brand-new Adidas Top Tens with the blue stripes; he loved the blue stripes. He then walked downstairs to meet what was left of the day.

First thing he saw was a note from his dad saying something about him mowing the lawn that day. He crumbled it up into a ball and tossed it in the trash. That was what was not going to happen.

Walking past the kitchen table, a newspaper article caught his eye, and so did the Post-it next to the obituary with the words, "Is this a friend of yours?" written on it. Franks name headlined the small obituary, and Freddie scanned it quickly. At the bottom of the obituary, it mentioned that it was an apparent suicide. Of course, Freddie knew differently, so did his friends and Jenny. But there was no way to prove it, so he brushed the thought from his mind.

The funeral was scheduled for 10:00 a.m., two days from now. Freddie knew he would attend but didn't know how he could look his friend's parents in the eyes, knowing that he had been the cause of his death. He figured he would tackle that problem when it came along. No reason to fret about it now.

Freddie stared out the window, looking at that 4Runner still sitting out there, wondering if anybody might come looking for it and not knowing if he would end up like his friend Frank.

Closing the newspaper, Freddie noticed a small story at the bottom of the front page. As he read, it described how a small Lear jet flight that originated from the Hillsboro Airport the day before had experienced some sort of problem over the Pacific Ocean. The debris field scattered for miles and was mostly made of partially burned and destroyed one hundred dollar bills. No owner to the jet could be traced, no black box had been recovered by printing time, and no cause had been mentioned. The last line of the story read, "The accident was still under investigation, outlook not good."

That answered his question. No one would be looking for this 4Runner. They went down in flames. Freddie said it out loud although no one else was around to hear it, "Thanks, Frank!" Then he went outside and mowed the lawn.

CHAPTER 58

On the other side of the country lived a news reporter/columnist for the *Washington Post*. Recently, he had been writing stories that alleged that the US government had been, for the past couple of years, engaging in illegal drug sales in the US, importing cocaine and selling it to the people that made up the inner city of the larger metropolitan areas of the United States then using the money made from those sales to line the pockets of Columbian drug lords and funding their secret wars in the countries of Iran and Nicaragua. Those stories are what had him placed on the Presidential Administrations undesirable list.

Most people would look at being on such a list as not being a good thing. However, Michael Johnson's eyes saw it differently than most. He had grown up in the inner city himself and was raised in a large family that, on more than one occasion, had been affected by the ravages that a crack addiction brought the family. Michael had lost his father, three brothers, and a sister to the prison system of Washington DC due to crimes committed either by selling drugs or trying to acquire drugs. The only other sibling he had, had been lost into the underbelly of the inner city's drug world. His mother and he himself figured they wouldn't hear from her until her body showed up in some morgue or in one of the many jail houses in the vicinity.

Michael Johnson, being the youngest, had felt the tragedy of the drugs in his life enough times that he had sworn to himself that he would do everything he could do to not only not be claimed as another victim of drugs but to do all he could to help rectify the situation. That's why he had become a reporter to bring the fight of the inner city into plain view, to shed some light on it and for the public to bear witness to.

Michael also had a selfish side to his reasons of being a big-time reporter on a big-time arena, and that was to break the big story, the story no one else had thought to investigate and, therefore, make himself a name, one that flowed from the lips of every American citizen. He not only wanted to break the news story of the century, but he also wanted to become the news himself. To be bigger than the stories he himself reported.

The end of the news day found Michael outside of his apartment complex, retrieving the day's mail from the banks of mailboxes located out by the street. As he flipped through the stack of mail, which consisted of the usual, stack of bills he found at this time every month. Reaching the bottom of the pile, he found a plain manila envelope postage marked Portland, Oregon. His curiosity grew, for he knew no one in Portland, Oregon, and the words "urgent" and "confidential" across the front of the envelope did nothing more than to make his curiosity grow even larger. He thumbed open the package while climbing the steps to his upper-floor apartment and fumbled to put the key into the lock of his front door while pulling out the only piece of paper he could find inside nested on top of the two Discs. He noticed right away they were not of the movie type but appeared to be computer-generated copies that would contain data more than entertainment. He read the note:

Dear Mister Johnson,

Who I am and where I got these discs is not important. What is important is that you know. I still have possession of the original and these are duplicate copies of the originals. I suspect that the contents on them will support all the speculation you have had concerning the government's role in the illegal drug trade and the money funding of wars denied by our government. Guard these discs closely and know that they may have cost the life of one person already.

There was no name, no signature at the bottom of the hand-written page, and there was no return address on the outside of the envelope.

Michael poured himself a drink and thought about the discs and the line in the letter stating that one death may have been caused by the discs already. It made him ask questions, questions like wouldn't someone know for sure if someone else was dead or not? And if this person had never seen what's on the discs, how could he know what's in them?

He decided to have another drink while contemplating what to do about the discs and also as a way to gain the courage to see what's on them. When he felt he was good and primed for what was to come next, he pulled out the discs, placed one in the tray of his laptop, and pushed the tray closed. It would only take a few minutes for the auto play to take over and reveal what was on the discs. The screen flashed and it read, "These discs are a matter of national security. Your computer will now shut down."

And then seconds later, his laptop shut down. As he sat there looking at his monitor in disbelief, in another building, a mere two blocks away, a buzzer buzzed loudly and a light flashed brightly.

In a matter of minutes, his apartment building was surrounded. Seconds later, his front door was breached, and minutes after that, you could hardly tell that anybody else had been there at all. In fact, when the body of Michael Johnson was found the next day after he didn't show up for work, the deadbolt on his front door was found locked from the inside just like all of his windows. The gun found in his hand would only have his fingerprints on it. No laptop or discs would be found.

Michael Johnson got his wish. The very next day he became part of the news he usually wrote. Apparent suicide is what it said on his short obituary written below his picture.

He was to be buried on the same day as Frank was to be buried. In fact, they were put into the ground and buried at the exact time, three time zones apart.

Two murders exact cause and under the same set of circum-stances. Both with two gunshot wounds to the head, both men's suicide was one of the worst cases of suicide that was known. Thousands of miles apart and evidence buried under six feet of soil, no dots would ever be connected; none could ever be proved.

CHAPTER 59

It was Saturday afternoon in late November, several months since all the action happened up on the hill. The three friends who had once been inseparable have yet to be seen together. They made themselves so scarce that it wouldn't surprise their friends and acquaintances if their names would soon grace the side of a milk carton.

Cliff and Lee lived in close proximity to one another and saw one another every once in a while and, upon occasion, would hang out together and maybe knock down a few beers today found them together. It was a typical November winter day in Hillsboro, Oregon. The current storm front began in mid-October and looked like it might blow over sometime in March or April. It was drizzling rainfall on a cloudy, gray day. As soon as they turned up on the driveway, they could see Freddie's metallic light blue Toyota 4Runner parked by the deck of the guest house, backed in looking like he was going to load something into the back of his SUV.

Cliff pulled the red racer into his side of the detached garage. His mothers' car sat on the other side and still had droplets of rain sitting on top of its paint. She hadn't been home all that long herself. All three of the boys were expecting this to be an awkward moment since it had been so long since they all found each other in the same room together. And the last time they did it was under extraordinary circumstances. That is if you count almost losing your life to Columbian mafia henchmen and a personal visit from the President of the United States of America extraordinary. A story they could share with no one because no one would ever believe it to be true.

Freddie was inside the guest house. For how long, they wouldn't know for sure, but the stack of empty beer cans gave them some idea—two, maybe three, hours.

"Nice 4Runner!" Cliff said as he walked in the front door. "Where did you pick that thing up at?"

"Thanks, you could say I picked it up down in Columbia." They all laughed.

The awkward moment they all expected melted away with a laugh and a big bear hug from Lee. Before they knew it, they had fallen into their places, or roles they had played for so many years in the past, back when they were mere boys. The events of last summer break surely allowed them to pass into manhood.

"What in the fuck are those old things doing in my house?" Cliff asked, pointing at the two old coolers that sat around the coffee table and which Freddy had been trying to bury in empty beer cans. "And why are there bows wrapped around them?" asked Cliff.

"First of all, your mom told me how Lee had puked all over the couch in late August, and that it had been sitting in the rain ever since, so I brought them in for something to sit on, and secondly, I ran into your dad a couple of weeks back, and I asked him about them, and he said I could have them nasty old things if I wanted them. As far as the bows go, I will get to that in a minute. Why don't you have a seat, and I will pack the first round of bong hits?

"That sounds like a good deal" Lee said. "So what happened to that old Dodge Dart? I figured you would be smashing that thing all across the country side," Freddie asked Lee.

"Hold on a second," Lee said and then took a big hit off of the bong. "I did mash it across the countryside and then I mashed it through old man Walkers barbed wire fence and then I smashed it into old man Walker's pond. Rumor has it I was chasing his cows around the pasture right before I ended up in the pond. They had to rescue me off the top of the Dodge Dart. I was naked, standing on top of it even though it was submerged with six inches of water over the top of it. Everyone says they are amazed I got out of the car alive!" Lee laughed as he finished. Freddie had been laughing through most of the story and started laughing again when Lee did.

"Now you know why we never let you have a turn at driving the Challenger or that shiny, new sports car." Freddie said.

Cliff was laughing now too and trying to hold down his bong hit, which made him laugh harder and that led to a bout of coughing..

They took to reminiscing like old friends, which of course they were. Each time one of them got close to anything about what happened that first week of summer break in 1983, a moment of silence would grip them, and someone would change the subject.

"How is Jenny doing?" Cliff finally asked. They all knew that this was a sore spot for all of them. There had been some underlying resentment about having to give up thirty million dollars for the girl Freddie would never get, but they all knew that even if it was sixty million, they still would have paid it.

"Well, right now I don't really know," Freddie said as he started again. His friends knew what would come next. "She had done found herself a new boyfriend a couple of months ago. I suppose I will hear something from her a couple of months from now once the big break takes place," he finished while looking down and shaking his head. At least he was no longer fooling himself by thinking he had a chance at her, his friends thought to themselves.

Silence overtook the room, and Cliff was the first one to break it and the first one to put it out there on the table so they could no longer hide from it nor dance around it.

"Thirty million fuckin' dollars!" Cliff said, and then let it hang in the room like a really bad fart for everyone to smell. "We had thirty million fuckin dollars in our hands for a full week, and all we came out with was a few fuckin pairs of tennis shoes!"

"Yeah, I know whatcha mean. I have nightmares where I have a shit load of money and then it always gets taken away right before I wake up!" Freddie replied.

"That brings me back to the bows being on those two coolers. Lee, you want to open those two fuckers up for me?"

"Sure," Lee said, standing up and off one of the coolers. Cliff stood up from the other one.

As the lids swung open, Freddie shouted, "Merry fucking Christmas!"

Both his friends stood there in complete silence, so Freddie continued, "I was only able to fit half of it in the coolers, or I would have grabbed more," Freddie said, now smiling from ear to ear and staring down with his friends at two coolers filled to the brim with bundles of fresh one hundred dollar bills.

"How in the fuck…," Lee trailed off and then became silent again.

"If you fellas have a few minutes, I will tell you all about it although by the look on Cliff's face, he is putting some of those pieces together right now."

"The morning I rode my bike up here, the same day shit hit the fan, I was able to stash half of the money in those two coolers, stuff the dry bags halfway with hay and put the money back on top. Sandwiched in one of them was the pipe bomb we built for the Berg's mailbox. Before I left Frank's that night, Frank and I rigged up an altimeter detonator that we attached to the pipe bomb."

Freddie threw the news article on the coffee table that reported the plane crash over the Pacific. Next he threw the *Washington Post* story of Michael Johnson's untimely suicide. I sent a copy of the discs to him but forgot to tell him not to have his computer hooked up to the Internet when he put them in it. He died the same way Frank died. You can thank Jenny for helping me piece this thing together. If she hadn't helped, we wouldn't be standing here with all of the loot."

Freddie stood up from his brand-new plastic cooler that was empty and said, "Why don't you guys peel off 2.5 million dollars from each cooler and drop it in mine to even out our cuts? Sorry, I had to keep it a secret from you, but I wanted to make sure nobody was going to come looking for it."

Freddie closed his cooler and then lowered it into the back of his 4Runner, and right after he jumped in, he yelled out his car window, "Give me a call next time you wanna go fishing!" Then all they could hear was his laughter as he drove away.

ABOUT THE AUTHOR

Edward Weil is a 49 year old long time resident of Hillsboro, Oregon. After battling a twenty-year addiction to methamphetamines which led him to five trips to rehabilitation programs as well as three visits in the Oregon Department of Corrections, he sat down and wrote "Sturgeon Point", his first novel. While awaiting sentencing to a 26-month prison sentence for a drug related crime, he wrote his book in eleven days using legal paper, and dozens of golf pencils. Inspired by events while growing up, Edward used memories of places, people, and events of his past and mixed in heavy doses of exaggeration, and embellishment to spin a tale of fiction. Free from his addiction to meth since November 15, 2012, Ed now works as a machine operator for a plastics parts manufacturing company in Hillsboro, Oregon.

CPSIA information can be obtained
at www.ICGtesting.com
Printed in the USA
FSOW01n0545110216
16754FS